'Gayle is back at his best'
Sun

Phil is thrilled that Helen has finally accepted his marriage proposal even if he practically bullied her into it. But before the big day there's one last ordeal to overcome: his stag weekend in Amsterdam.

Even with his mates all pushing forty it's guaranteed to be less about clogs and tulips and more about getting off their faces and trawling bars for girls. But when Phil gets talking to one such girl everything changes: not because he fancies her, or because she's pretty, but because they have so much in common, even if neither of them knows it yet.

And then of course there's what the girls are up to at their luxury spa hotel...

Told as two separate stories that have implications for both Helen and Phil's future happiness, *The Stag and Hen Weekend* is a fresh and original story of a couple trying to get it right and all too often getting it spectacularly wrong.

Mike Gayle is the author of ten bestselling novels and has contributed to a variety of magazines including *FHM*, *Sunday Times Style* and *Cosmopolitan*.

Also by Mike Gayle

My Legendary Girlfriend
Mr Commitment
Turning Thirty
Dinner for Two
His 'n' Hers
Brand New Friend
Wish You Were Here
Life and Soul of the Party
The Importance of being a Bachelor
Men at Work – Quick Read

Non-fiction

The To-Do List

THE STAG WEEKEND

MIKE GAYLE

HODDER

First published in Great Britain in 2012 by Hodder & Stoughton
An Hachette UK company

First published in paperback in 2013

1

A CIP catalogue record for this title is available from the British Library

ISBN 978 1 444 70860 8 (B format)
ISBN 978 1 444 76855 8 (A format)

Printed and bound by Clays Ltd, St Ives plc

Hodder & Stoughton policy is to use papers that are natural, renewable and recyclable products and made from wood grown in sustainable forests. The logging and manufacturing processes are expected to conform to the environmental regulations of the country of origin.

Hodder & Stoughton Ltd
338 Euston Road
London NW1 3BH

www.hodder.co.uk

For the girls

Acknowledgements

Thanks to Simon Trewin and all at United Agents, Steve Brayford (for research duties), Chris McCabe, Merel van Beeren (for the Dutch lessons), and above all, to C, for pretty much everything.

Friday

1.

'Shouldn't you be packing?'

Phil Hudson furtively covered the open notepad in which he had been scribbling at the kitchen counter with a nearby tea towel and swivelled around on his stool to face his fiancée.

'When did you come in?' he asked as she stared intently at him from the doorway, two carrier bags of shopping in her hands.

'Just now.'

'I didn't hear you.'

Helen eyed Phil suspiciously. 'You weren't meant to. And just so you know, once we're married be prepared to see more of me popping up in places you aren't expecting me to be. I'll be everywhere. I promise you.' Having clearly amused herself, she chuckled and set down the bags on the table. 'What were you doing anyway? Isn't the boy Simon meant to be picking you up at ten?'

'That's what he said.'

'So you're all packed?'

'I made a start but couldn't find half the stuff I needed. I think we need a system.'

'A system?'

'Yeah, a system, you know, so that we both know where stuff is without having to ask.'

'We already have a system you big goon!' snapped Helen. 'How do you think I find the things we need every day? What you actually mean is that *you* don't understand the system because whenever I try and explain it, you do that thing that I hate where you make out you're listening but are in fact doing the opposite.'

'Like when?'

'Like when what?'

'Like when wasn't I listening?'

'Er . . . let me think . . . perhaps it was the last time you told me that we needed a system! Or the time before that, oh and the time before that too!'

Fun though it was, Phil reasoned that he had probably wound Helen up enough for the day and so applying his best cheeky chap grin, he walked over, put his arms around her waist and kissed her. 'But you love me really don't you? he said, approximating a suitably coquettish eyelash flutter.

'You know I do,' she smiled, 'but don't think for a minute that it's a get-out-of-jail-free card, okay?'

'Wouldn't dream of it.'

'Good.'

Phil started to rummage through the carrier bags. 'What have you bought? Anything nice?'

Helen shrugged. 'Nothing much. Just a few bits and bobs to make sandwiches.'

Phil plucked out a packet of pre-sliced Gouda cheese. 'Sandwiches for what?'

Clearly embarrassed Helen snatched the cheese from Phil leaving him to answer his own question. The penny dropped. 'You're planning to make sandwiches for me aren't you?'

Helen glowered.

'You do realise,' began Phil, 'that making sandwiches for me to take on my stag do is adorable, don't you? I mean it's something a Disney character might do, if, say, Disney characters' fiancés were the type to go on stag dos to Amsterdam. Right now you should have cartoon bluebirds flying around your head and animated squirrels at your feet.'

Helen scowled. 'You don't have to have them if you don't want them,' she said narrowing her eyes at him. 'I could just as easily put it all in the bin if you're going to be all smart-arsey about it!'

Phil once again took Helen in his arms and kissed the top of her head in a manner he hoped she would interpret as playfully patronising rather than, as it was, a demonstration of his deepest and most true affection for her. He loved this woman, and the idea that she was going to be his wife thrilled him to his core. 'Smart-arsey? Me? Never. Of course I'll take them. I'll take them and proudly eat them on the plane and when all the boys are mocking me mercilessly I will ignore their abuse secure in the knowledge that while their other halves – if they have them – have sent them to Amsterdam without so much as a KitKat, mine has kitted me out with . . .' Phil paused while he checked the contents of the carrier bags, 'Wagon Wheels, satsumas, ham, a large packet of Starburst and . . .' he paused glancing over at the confiscated cheese, 'let's not forget Gouda sandwiches. You are undoubtedly a nutter, my sweet, but I honestly would not – for a single second – want you any other way.'

Helen reluctantly kissed Phil and then set about unpacking the bags. As she turned her back in order to put some of the shopping in the fridge, Phil retrieved the notebook from under the tea towel and tossed it casually on top of a pile of magazines on the counter next to the microwave.

'So,' said Helen returning from her trip to the fridge. 'What were you doing in here?'

'Doing?'

'Yes,' she replied as though Phil was hard of hearing, 'doing. As in "What were you doing in here when I came in?" '

'I wasn't *doing* anything,' said Phil. 'I came in for a glass of water and stayed a moment or two to ponder the nature of my own mortality.'

'Where's the glass?'

Phil stared at the counter as if expecting to see the glass that he knew full well wasn't there. 'Oh, that, I washed it up.'

'You're telling me you came into the kitchen, poured yourself a glass of water, drank the water and *then* washed up the glass?'

Phil maintained an air of innocence even though it was apparent that he had been well and truly caught out.

'Now I know you're lying. You've never used a glass and washed it up straight away in the entire time we've been together. What's going on?'

Any excuse Phil might have offered would be torn apart by Helen in a matter of seconds, but he was saved by the sound of his mobile phone's ringtone – one more suited to signalling to the crew of a World War Two battleship to man battle stations.

'Hey you,' said a female voice. 'I'm at work. Got a full day ahead but I just thought I'd check in before you get off.'

Helen silently mouthed: 'Who is it?' in his direction and he mouthed 'Caitlin' in reply. Helen's response was to go cross-eyed, stick her tongue out and mime self-strangulation.

For reasons that Phil had never been one hundred per cent sure of, Helen and his younger sister Caitlin had never got on. Yes, maybe in the vague realms of the past there had been some hard feelings over him choosing to go out with Helen instead of reuniting with his sister's friend Beth, but that had been a long time ago. Even with insider knowledge of the women with whom he had shared his life, Phil couldn't believe a regular human being could hold a grudge that long. There must be something more to their antagonism, something on one level to do with him but on another nothing to do with him at all, and everything to do with some kind of mysterious feminine primeval power play.

'Hey, sis! How's it going?' said Phil seizing the opportunity to take both himself and his conversation out of the kitchen and into the hallway. 'All ready and packed for your weekend of luxury in Ashbourne?'

'Did it all last night but I'm actually not due to arrive until Saturday morning.'

'How come?'

'Too much on at work.'

'But aren't all the other girls arriving tonight?'

Caitlin sighed. 'Come on Phil, you know what Friday night traffic is like. Plus, I've got a hair appointment, sort of a pre-wedding job. Got to look good for those photos!'

Phil didn't laugh.

'What?'

'You know.'

Caitlin tutted loudly. 'Not this again! I've promised that I'll try harder with her. Isn't that enough?'

'Well actually, no,' snapped Phil glancing over at the kitchen door, 'not unless you follow through with it.' He lowered his voice. 'Look, Helen inviting you on her hen weekend is her way of saying that she wants to make a fresh start. Surely the least you could do is meet her halfway by not turning up late for her hen weekend?'

'Listen to yourself!' snapped Caitlin. 'She's got you so wrapped around her little finger that you don't even know it! Less than a couple of minutes into what was supposed to be a pleasant phone call to wish you well for the weekend it's an argument with you taking her side over mine!'

Phil had heard this accusation many times before and he was having none of it. 'Oh come off it Cait, what are you, six? It's not a question of me taking sides. I just want the two of you to get along, that's all. This time next week, whether you like it or not, she'll be family and I want you both to make the effort.'

'So you'll be giving her a stern talking to as well I hope?'

Exhausted at the prospect of this war between Caitlin and Helen carrying on throughout his married life Phil sat down on the stairs and rubbed his eyes. He didn't want to be having this conversation so early in the morning and certainly not at the beginning of a weekend that would see his fiancée and his sister spending the weekend together without him present to act as referee. He needed to make peace with Caitlin if only because it fell to him as her older brother to lead by example. 'Look, I'm sorry, okay? You're right. I shouldn't have doubted you. You turn up when you can and I'll keep my big nose out of it. So are we good?'

'Of course we are,' reassured Caitlin. 'We're always good. So come on then, tell me more about your plans for the weekend. How raucous is it going to be? Bit different from Helen's weekend.'

'It's a stag do in Amsterdam,' sighed Phil, 'How good can it be?'

'You're not looking forward to it?'

'It's not that. It's just I'd rather stay at home.'

'But I thought it was going to be a no strip clubs, no coffee houses, strictly classy affair.'

'That's how it was sold to me. But you know what the

boys are like. On their own they're fine but together they're experts at whipping each other into a frenzy. Put them in a place like Amsterdam and well . . . pretty much anything could happen.'

They talked for a while longer about arrangements for the wedding but Phil's heart wasn't in it. Ending the call with one last plea to Caitlin to be on her best behaviour, Phil returned to the kitchen where Helen was standing over a chopping board making the very sandwiches for which he had earlier mocked her.

'What's up with the little princess now?'

'Nothing,' said Phil leaning on the granite counter top, 'she was ringing to wish me well for the weekend. She sends her love by the way.'

Helen rolled her eyes. 'I bet she does,' she said sarcastically. 'Is it too late to beg you to take her with you? I'm sure the boys won't mind having someone as glamorous as your sister about.'

'I couldn't think of anything worse. It's all I can do to stop them drooling over her whenever they see her.'

'Well, she's coming with me so you're safe on that score. Not that any of your mates would be up to her usual standard anyway. What was it the last one did for a living?'

'I don't think he actually *did* anything,' replied Phil. 'He was always whisking her off somewhere exotic in a bid to impress her, seemingly oblivious that when it comes to blokes my sister takes being unimpressed to such a high level that it's practically an art form.'

Helen sliced through the sandwiches she had just

made and looked up at Phil. 'Do you think she'll ever settle down?'

'Who knows?' said Phil helping himself to a sliver of pre-sliced Gouda. 'Maybe if she bags herself a minor royal. But until then I think it'll strictly be the handsome and the unattainably rich that do it for her.' He took a huge bite from the cheese, chewed and then folded up the remains and dropped it into his mouth.

'You'll give yourself indigestion,' said Helen moving the cheese out of reach.

'Maybe,' said Phil, 'but the thought of you and Caitlin carrying on the way you do is absolutely guaranteed to do so.'

'So that was what the call was about? Her complaining about me? What am I supposed to have done now? Dared to breathe while in her presence?'

Phil walked over to Helen and put his arms around her. 'Come on you, I know she's a pain in the arse sometimes, I know you haven't exactly got much in common but will you find a way to make this weekend work? Just for me? I don't know whether it's that I won't be there to pull the two of you apart if it comes to blows, but I've got a horrible feeling that this weekend is going to be make or break for you.'

'It'll be fine,' said Helen. She kissed his neck. 'I promise, I'll be on my best behaviour and no matter what she says or does I won't let her get to me.'

Chuckling to himself, Phil sneaked a final slice of cheese and retreated to the bedroom to recommence packing for the weekend.

2.

Phil dropped three pairs of Calvin Klein briefs into the bag and hovered over it staring at them. Were three pairs of pants enough to cover all manner of potential underwear emergencies? Deciding to err on the side of caution he added an extra pair and then picked up his trainers from the floor and dropped them in too. A couple of pairs of socks were next, then he walked over to the wardrobe and picked out three white shirts, three casual tops and his favourite jeans. Placing them on the left-hand side of the bag, he picked up the sheet of paper that had been lying on the opposite side and began to read.

The print-out in his hand was an email Simon, his best man, had sent to everyone listing everything needed for the weekend. Phil had received the list earlier in the week and had scrutinised it carefully in an attempt to deduce what its contents might reveal about the secret plans his friend had organised for the weekend. The list included: 'clothes suitable for an outdoor sporting activity', 'a valid UK driver's licence', 'enough Euros to cover two days of solid drinking', and a demand that everyone should sort out some form of insurance because 'A guaranteed way to put a dampener on the whole weekend is to have to fork out for a medical helicopter out of the beer kitty when one of us knocks himself unconscious.' The stand out item on the list, however, (written in bold with certain sections highlighted with capitals for added emphasis) was the mention of a black suit, black tie and at least three white shirts. Phil had emailed Simon to find out the reasoning behind these items and was rebuffed with the not altogether reassuring response of: 'All will become clear.'

Phil tossed the list back on to the bed and continued packing. He grabbed a final pair of briefs before making his way to the bathroom for a shower.

While he waited for the water to warm up he looked at his watch. A week and a day from this exact moment he would be getting ready for his wedding. He swallowed hard at the thought but when he looked up at the mirror in front of him, he had a huge grin on his face.

Half an hour later, showered, shaved and dressed, Phil, feeling not unlike a secret agent and/or contract killer in his black suit and tie, descended the stairs carrying his weekend suitcase to the sound of raucous laughter from his best man.

'And here he is! The man of the hour!' trumpeted Simon as the two men exchanged man hugs. 'Are you all ready fella?'

'As I'll ever be.'

Helen looked Phil and Simon up and down. 'What do

you two look like in those suits? Are you going to tell me what the whole get up thing is all about?'

Phil shrugged. 'You're asking the wrong man.'

'My attempt to set the right tone for the weekend,' explained Simon. 'Amsterdam is going to be full of boys doing the stag weekend thing. But we'll be the only ones working the *Reservoir Dogs* look the whole time.'

Phil laughed. 'And the only ones arguing about who's not going to be Mr Pink – which given it's my stag do is most certainly not going to be me.'

'Si was just telling me the story of the stag night you organised for him back in the day,' said Helen. 'Apparently you didn't need themes back then. Just beer money and an evil imagination. I can't believe how awful you lot were to him.'

'We were young and over excited,' explained Phil. 'He was the first of our lot to get married. To be fair I actually think he got off quite lightly.'

'It's true,' said Simon. 'My middle brother got hitched the year after me and his mates practically tortured him for the whole of his stag do. At one point they were threatening to strip him naked and abandon him in the middle of Brighton and it was only when I intervened that they settled for shaving off one of his eyebrows instead. You should see his wedding photos – they are the funniest things ever – I think some of them are on YouTube if you can be bothered to look for them. One of his mates uploaded them as an anniversary present a few years ago and put them on a video set to the music of Johnny Cash. Even now whenever I hear the opening bars of "I Walk the Line" I'm practically doubled over with laughter just thinking about his face with a drawn-on eyebrow. He looked like one of the missing Marx Brothers! His missus went mental and didn't talk to any of us for a good half year after the big day.'

Helen threw Simon a wary glance. 'I take it you've got all that out of your system now? It's not like you're in your twenties any more.'

'True,' sighed Simon. 'More's the shame. I could do with a laugh.'

Phil raised an eyebrow. 'Everything okay?'

Simon shrugged. 'Got a lot on at work. It'll all get sorted but it's just a bit of a pain in the arse when you're stuck in the middle of it. Anyway, nothing could put a dampener on this weekend. And I do mean nothing. I don't want to oversell it, mate, but if this weekend doesn't make it into your all-time top ten great times I will happily resign as your best man and let Degsy take the lead role.'

'Well,' Helen butted in, 'it better had be the weekend of your life because I promise there is no way that I'm going to let Degsy have anything to do with the main ceremony. He's not all there, that boy.'

Phil protested. 'That's a bit harsh, babe. He's just a bit special that's all.'

'The last time I saw him he licked the inside of an ash tray because one of you lot bet him that he wouldn't.'

'And that makes him not all there? He's just a man who likes a challenge.'

'Well, challenge or not, he's not going to be your best man. There's no knowing what he'd do.'

Phil looked at Simon. 'She's right you know. A lot of family and friends would have to die before I'd even consider him and even then I'd still pick a total stranger over him much as I love the guy.'

'Cool,' said Simon, 'then it looks like I'm going to have to stick to my word and pull off the single most amazing weekend of your life.'

'No pressure there then.'

'None at all.'

Phil and Simon first met each other back when they were teenagers working as Saturday sales assistants in Sharper Sounds, a Hi-Fi shop in the middle of Derby city centre. Phil hadn't been all that keen on Simon to begin with mainly because Simon had seemed so much more different from himself than most people he knew. Simon spoke with what to Phil sounded like a posh accent, lived in a big house over in Strutts Park and went to a nearby grammar school while Phil spoke with a Derby accent, attended a local comprehensive and lived on the Brandswood estate where pretty much every shop bar the local chip shop had grilles over their windows. And although they had shared many things from music through to the kinds of girls they found attractive Phil couldn't imagine how they might ever become friends who saw each other out of the shop, but that's exactly what they did.

Years later when Carl, the owner of Sharper Sounds announced that he was putting the shop up for sale the two men went to the pub to discuss the news.

'You should buy the lease and take over,' suggested the recently graduated Simon. 'I'll help you put together a business plan. It'll be a doddle.'

'Thanks but no thanks,' replied Phil who in the intervening years had worked his way up to assistant manager of the shop. 'It's too big a risk. I've seen the books, you have no idea how close the shop has come to closing in the past.'

Knowing that owning the shop had always been Phil's dream, Simon refused to take no for an answer and Phil finally caved in, funnelling all his savings and those of his mum into a year-long lease. Within six months of signing the paperwork he produced the most profitable financial quarter in the shop's twenty-two-year history.

Phil in return had over the years been equally as good a friend to him, not only bailing finance manager Simon out of his innumerable scrapes and situations brought on by his own recklessness, but he was also responsible for introducing him to Yaz, the woman who would one day become his wife.

At the time in question Phil and Simon had both been single and desperate for a holiday, and so when Simon had suggested that they should both book a week off work and fly off somewhere warm Phil had leaped at the chance, and within a short space of time they found themselves heading off for a last-minute break to Crete.

On their first night out at the resort while sitting in a bar near their hotel that overlooked the beach Simon spotted two girls walk in, one of whom he claimed to be the most beautiful girl he had ever seen.

'You should talk to her,' encouraged Phil. 'What's the worst that could happen?'

'I could find out that she's going to start work at my place and have to sit opposite her in meetings all day,' replied Simon who had recently had his confidence knocked after being turned down by someone he fancied at work.

With no other option available Phil did the only thing he could think of and downed the remains of his beer glass, walked over to the girls and making it clear to Yaz that he was interested in her friend, talked the girls into joining him and Simon for a drink at a different bar further along the strip.

Three bars and a visit to a nightclub called the Frisky Palace later and Simon was getting on like a house on fire with Yaz, and things continued in that vein on their return home to England. After five years and a move for Phil from Derby to Nottingham they were getting engaged and throwing a party to celebrate, an event which in itself would change Phil's life because it was there that he met Helen for the first time.

'Right,' said Simon setting his empty mug down in the sink. 'I think we should probably be getting off. I know it doesn't take that long to get to the airport but I got caught out a few weeks ago trying to catch a flight to

Düsseldorf because of a pile-up two junctions before the motorway exit. Missed the flight, the next one wasn't until early afternoon and that was fully booked so I ended up having to travel the following day and staying twice as long to reschedule all the meetings I'd missed.'

Phil laughed. 'To be fair, mate, the way you've been talking up this weekend I'd be more than a bit relieved to miss the flight. Right now the idea of being stuck in Nottingham for the weekend is looking pretty attractive.'

Simon shook his head in dismay. 'You, my friend, are the queen of old ladies. I promise you, sunshine, this'll be the last time I'm lowering my standards to be your best man.'

'I should hope so,' said Helen. She hugged Phil tightly. 'I mean it Simon,' she said looking stern. 'I will hunt you down like a dog if anything . . . and I do mean anything *at all* untoward happens to Phil. He might not look like it on the outside but he's a sensitive soul so just go easy on him, okay?'

Simon was about to hug Helen goodbye when Phil's phone rang.

'Probably work,' said Phil reaching for his phone.

'More likely Degsy calling from the wrong airport wondering where we all are.'

Phil glanced down at the screen. 'Looks like we're both wrong. It's my dad.'

It had been weeks since Phil had last spoken to Patrick Hudson, and even that was only because he had dialled the wrong number. It wasn't so much that Phil and his dad didn't get on. They got on well enough given that in Phil's twenties they'd gone the best part of four years without talking. It was more that Phil had long since grown tired of waiting for his sixty-six-year-old frequently absent, philandering, former rock-band roadie of a father to grow up.

'Dad,' said Phil making his way into the hallway and sitting on the exact same stair where he had earlier spoken to his sister. 'What's up?'

'All right, son? Just thought I'd check in and see how you are.'

'I'm fine, Dad. You?'

'Never better. How's that fiancée of yours? She good?'

'She's great, Dad.'

'You've got a special one there, you know that don't you? Don't cock it all up by being Jack the lad now will you?'

It was too good a line to pass up. 'You mean like you did with Mum?'

'That was different, son. And you know it.'

Phil sighed and looked at his watch. He didn't want to have this argument again, especially as the last half dozen times it had ended with one or other of them putting the phone down mid-conversation.

'Fine,' said Phil. 'Look, Dad, I was actually just heading out the door. I got your reply to the wedding invite the other day so I'm assuming you're still all right to come.'

'Wouldn't miss it for the world!'

'I'm pleased to hear it.'

'So where are you off to in such a rush?'

'Amsterdam, Dad, it's my stag do.'

'Amsterdam! Now there's a city that knows how to party. I remember being there back in the early seventies for a European tour with this American rock band who were tipped to be the next Iron Butterfly. The night after their first gig I fell asleep in a hotel room and woke up in a tree in a park! A tree! No idea how I'd got there and even less of an idea how I'd managed to sleep. Nearly missed the coach taking us on to Belgium too!' He chuckled, a deep throaty laugh of the variety that sounded more insincere than heart-warming. 'Those were the days, I tell you. What I wouldn't give to be twenty-five again.'

'Yeah well,' said Phil, who had heard the story many times before, 'when you find a way of doing that, let me know and I'll do the marketing for you.'

'And we'll make a fortune,' said Patrick wistfully.

Phil ran out of patience. 'And so the thing that you called me up for was . . .'

'Do you have to be so brutal?'

'I'm not, Dad, I just want you to get to the point that's all. I've got a plane to catch.'

'Fine,' snapped Patrick. 'I could do with a little extra help this month.'

'Don't tell me you've got through it already?'

'I was a bit short last month – couple of unexpected bills – and it's had a knock-on effect that's all. I'll pay you back, every last cent, on that you have my word. Haven't checked last week's lottery numbers yet but I've got a good feeling about them.'

'How much?'

'Five hundred would take the edge off.'

'Fine.'

'But if you could make it six that would be even better. And you'll get it back. Scout's honours and all that.'

'Fine,' said Phil. 'I'll get the money moved to your account first thing Monday, okay?'

'That's brilliant son,' said Patrick. 'You're a good boy, you know that?'

'Yeah,' sighed Phil. 'I'm pretty sure I'm the best.'

Phil returned his phone to his pocket and picked up his bag from the floor in the hallway. 'Come on then, Si,' he called into the kitchen. 'Let's go if we're going.'

'You seem annoyed,' said Helen as they made their way to the front door. 'What did your dad want?'

'The usual.'

Helen squeezed his hand. 'I'm sorry, sweetheart. I know he can be a pain sometimes but you shouldn't let him get you down. This is your weekend and you need to make the most of it.'

'And I will,' said Phil. He kissed her one last time. 'You take care, okay? Have a great time and I'll see you back here on Sunday night.'

3.

It was quarter to eleven as Phil and Simon disembarked from the airport shuttle bus in front of the large revolving doors at the entrance to East Midlands Airport. The last time Phil had been here, he and Helen had flown to Madrid for a long weekend over the May Day bank holiday and getting Helen to marry him seemed about as unlikely as him learning to speak Spanish. Some three years later he was back, about to fly to Amsterdam for his own stag do.

Once through the revolving doors, the boys looked up at the screens above their heads for flight information.

'That's us,' said Simon pointing. 'Flight 368 to Amsterdam checking in at desks 16 to 18.'

Phil nodded but didn't say anything, which was no great change since he'd barely spoken since Helen had waved them off from the house. Reasoning that whatever was bothering him would come out sooner or later, Simon had left his friend to his brooding, content to allow the radio to keep him company.

Taking the lead Simon scanned their surroundings and parked Phil at the end of the queue for the check-in desk. Simon checked the queue and then double-checked the surrounding areas for the boys in case (though this would be a highly unlikely scenario) any of them had arrived on time. No sign.

'You okay?' asked Simon as a trendy looking couple joined the queue behind them. 'You hardly said a word on the way over.'

Suddenly conscious of his own reticence, Phil sighed, rubbing his eyes as though he'd just woken from a deep sleep. 'Yeah, I'm fine, mate, really. It's just I've got a few things on my mind that's all.'

'Your dad?'

'He's one of them.'

'What's he up to now?'

'Nothing new. I just wish . . . I don't know . . . I just wish he was like other dads, that's all. Why couldn't he be more like your old man?'

'You wouldn't want my old man for a father believe me,' said Simon warily. 'Never had a decent conversation with him in my life. At least your old man's lived a little and you can have a laugh with him. I'm not even sure I've seen my dad smile.'

Phil wasn't convinced. 'He's not that bad. A bit reserved maybe but at least he was always around.'

'A bit too much if you ask me,' replied Simon, 'but I get what you're saying. Still, for all his faults no one can tell a story like your old man, can they? Only last week I was telling a couple of guys from work that story about him going to bed in a hotel in Amsterdam and waking up in a tree in a park. Don't you think he'd be great to have on the stag weekend?'

'My dad? Are you mental? He'd be a nightmare.'

Simon looked crestfallen. 'Really?'

'Yes, really,' replied Phil. 'You'd never know what hare-brained scheme he'd be working on. I'd never relax. And as for that ridiculous anecdote – which I'm pretty sure he made up – he told it to me again less than an hour ago.' Exhausted at the very thought of his dad Phil rubbed his eyes with his fists. 'I'm just sick of bailing him out that's all. If he hadn't been waking up in trees or running off to the Far East with whichever band he was working for at the time then maybe he wouldn't have to come to me for handouts every five minutes.'

Simon placed a reassuring hand on his friend's shoulder. 'It must be tough mate but I'm sure he appreciates it.'

Yeah,' said Phil, 'I'm sure he does in his own way.' He looked at Simon. 'This weekend: it's not going to be just drinking and dodgy clubs is it?'

Simon laughed. 'You make it sound so sordid when you say it like that.'

'You know what I mean,' said Phil. 'I'm as up for a laugh as the next man but it seems a bit of a waste coming all the way out here just to drink beer and watch bored couples have soulless sex for public consumption.' Phil laughed. 'If that's what you're after we could save ourselves the airfare, nip into town at throwing out time and stand outside the Ritzy.'

Simon eyed his friend suspiciously. 'Are you saying you want to visit an art gallery or two while we're out there? It's a stag do, not a school trip!'

'And don't I know it! All I'm saying is, given that I've never been there before, I wouldn't mind actually seeing some of it if the opportunity comes up.'

'Well if it does I'll let you know, okay?' said Simon, 'But I'm pretty sure there won't be enough time. Anyway, to be honest mate you're not missing much. I went there when I was a student and it wasn't all that. Okay, so there's Van Gogh and his Sunflowers, Anne Frank's house, tulips, clogs, Edam and a bunch of canals. But let's face it, even back when pretending to be "into" culture might have got you the girl, the best thing about the place was getting off your face and checking out the red-light area. Say what you like about Amsterdam as a city of culture, but any place where you can smoke pot *and* drink world class beer has got to be the number one destination for a stag do. It's the Las Vegas of Europe, only without any annoying Yanks to take the edge off things.'

Phil laughed. 'I've known you way too long to think for a minute that you're that ignorant.'

'People change,' said Simon shrugging. 'You might not like it. They might not like it. But it happens all the time.'

The queue surged forward as a large extended family featuring at least four different generations was beckoned to the check-in desk. Phil and Simon picked up their bags and moved forwards to take up the slack and yet another silence descended.

Simon nudged his friend in the overly jocular fashion that a schoolboy might try to coax another schoolboy out of a black mood. 'So, come on then, what else is on your mind?'

Phil frowned. He was sure that he'd snap out of his mood soon but all this attention really wasn't helping matters. 'How do you mean?'

'You said you had a few things on your mind. Unless I've miscounted your dad is only one.'

'Well, the other is my kid sister.'

'Caitlin? What's she done?'

'Nothing *yet*,' replied Phil, 'but that could have changed by Monday morning. Helen invited her to the hen weekend.'

'Oh that,' said Simon. 'I thought she was winding you up with something new. That spat with Helen's been going on for ages hasn't it? Why are you suddenly worried about it now?'

'Because this is different,' said Phil. 'Normally I'm around to referee before the claws come out but who knows what'll happen without me there? I can feel it in my gut. Trouble is brewing. Caitlin can be pretty bitchy when she wants to be and Helen . . . well once she gets her back up . . .'

Simon laughed. 'Remember that time when the four of us went to V festival and that drunk bird kept deliberately bumping into her?' Simon winced comically. 'Now that was a tongue-lashing and a half! I bet that girl gets flashbacks even now!'

'Exactly,' said Phil, 'so imagine what it would be like being at the receiving end of a tongue-lashing that's been eight years in the making.' Simon did his comedy wince again and this time it provoked the beginnings of a smile. 'See what I mean? It's too much to even contemplate.'

'Still,' he continued, 'I can't imagine Caitlin getting into anything with Helen the week before the wedding. It's too important.'

Phil grudgingly conceded his friend's point. 'I suppose not. If they did my mum would have a right go at the pair of them.'

'How's Caitlin doing anyway?' asked Simon. 'Haven't seen her for a while.'

'You know her,' said Phil, 'she's always fine. Whether it's being the only girl from our school to get into grammar school or the first member of the family to go to university, that girl always lands on her feet.'

'She seeing any one?'

Phil studied his friend. 'Why the interest? You're not trying to palm that idiot brother of yours off on her again are you?'

'Have you any idea how much that "idiot" is making these days as a fully qualified barrister? Only last week he was telling me how he was test driving a Ferrari!'

'And you think that would impress Caitlin? Honestly, mate, you have no idea of the kind of guy she goes for. I wouldn't be surprised if she turned up with a proper "A" list celebrity the next time we go to Mum and Brian's for Sunday lunch. She's done the rich thing, now she wants them rich *and* famous.'

Before Simon could reply there was a sharp tug on his trousers and they were halfway down his thighs exposing his expensive designer underwear to the world. Frantically pulling up his trousers he spun around angrily to see Reuben, Deano, Spencer and Degsy (all dressed in black suits and ties) bent double in hysterics.

'Do that again and I'll knock you out,' threatened Simon in a doomed attempt to wrest back his dignity.

'Mate,' sniggered Deano, 'it was just too good an opportunity to pass up. You know we love you really.'

'Yeah, I bet,' replied Simon peering over Deano's shoulder. 'And right now there's a copper with a high-vis vest coming this way who looks like he wants in on the joke.'

A look of horror spread across their faces, all the more amusing for the lack of an actual policeman. Suitably chastened Deano and the boys immediately shed their adolescent skin and acting more like grown men who had jobs, mortgages and responsibilities, joined Phil and Simon in the queue.

Phil had known them all in one capacity or another for years. Reuben had been one of Simon's oldest friends from school and as such had inevitably become one of Phil's closest friends too. Spencer was the former assistant manager of Phil's Nottingham store who now worked as a rep for an electronic goods distribution company and had recently separated from his long-term girlfriend. Deano was an old friend from the cricket team Phil used to play with back in his early twenties who along with his ex-wife ran the Horses, an up-market pub and bistro that the six friends often frequented. And finally Degsy was Phil's oldest school friend who, having followed many different career paths over the years, was currently trying his hand at painting and decorating while trying to win back the mother of his two kids. All six were part of an irregular five-a-side (it was a rare week if all six of them turned up at the same time) team called the Beeston Wanderers who played once a week at the local sports centre.

After what felt like a lifetime they finally reached the front of the queue and one by one checked on to the flight. En route to the departure gate they were all casually engaged in separate conversations with Phil and Spencer chatting about work, Deano and Simon talking about a couple of films Simon had watched and Degsy and Reuben talking football, but before they reached the escalator that would take them up through to security Simon called them all to one side.

'This is like school trips used to be back in the day!' whined Degsy. 'What's up now headmaster?'

Simon pulled out a Tesco carrier bag from his rucksack and theatrically dropped his phone in it. 'This is what's up.'

Reuben laughed. 'Are you going to do a trick?'

'Nope,' said Phil reading his friend's mind. 'I think he wants us all to hand over our phones.'

Reuben made it clear that he wasn't going to comply. 'No, can do,' he said firmly. 'I told the missus she'd be able to call me any time.'

'Which is exactly why I want us all to leave them behind,' said Simon. 'I know it's a pain in the arse, but this weekend won't be the same if we're all tied to our phones for the whole of it.'

'You just don't want us uploading pictures of your hairy backside to Facebook!' retorted Reuben.

'No mate,' replied Simon, 'what I actually don't want is to spend the whole weekend watching you yakking to your missus on the phone.'

'Like that would happen.'

'I've seen it with my own eyes! The last time we went to see County play. You spent more time looking at your phone than you did watching the game!'

'We just like to keep in touch that's all.'

'More she just likes to keep a track of where you are and what you're doing. Why don't you go the full hog and get yourself a GPS device fitted?'

'Si's right,' said Deano dropping his phone into the bag. 'I went on a stag do last summer and it was a real drag. You'd be there trying to have a laugh and every five minutes some guy would be taking a call, sending a text or wandering around the pub looking for a signal.'

'Cool,' said Simon, 'so that's two down.' He jiggled the bag in Phil's direction. 'Come on mate, you know it makes sense.'

Phil looked at the bag blankly. While he didn't normally feel the need to text home as often as it appeared Reuben did, he did during the normal course of a day like to send Helen at least one or two just to say hello, even more so when he had to go away overnight on business. The idea of not communicating with Helen for the best part of three whole days was disconcerting and if it had been any other group of people in any other situation he wouldn't even have contemplated it. But these were his closest friends who, even though some, like Degsy, weren't exactly flush with cash, hadn't so much as raised an eyebrow at the expense involved simply because it was his stag do.

'Okay, I'm in,' said Phil dropping his mobile into the bag. 'Let's keep it old school.'

'Me too,' said Degsy.

'A pre-Nokia world it is then,' said Spencer with a stoic raise of the eyebrow before adding his to the bag.

'You guys don't get it,' implored Reuben, 'my missus will do her nut if she can't get hold of me all weekend. She once couldn't get hold of me for a day because I'd left my charger at home and by the time I got back from work she'd practically packed her bags.'

'Mate,' said Simon holding out his hand, 'you're embarrassing yourself. Just give me the phone.'

'Just know this,' said Reuben looking at Phil as he dropped his phone in the bag, 'you owe me big time.'

Clutching the bag of phones Simon disappeared in search of a left luggage locker and returned some twenty minutes later just as a message came over the tannoy: "Could passengers Dean, Corrbridge, Collins, Hudson, McDonald and Brayford please come to gate 11 immediately where flight 368 to Amsterdam is ready to depart."

Not needing to be told twice the boys ran full pelt along the corridor to security while Simon went into a long explanation of why it had taken him the best part of half an hour to leave the bag of phones at the left luggage counter which involved staffing problems and a malfunctioning credit card reader. Once they were through to the other side, they were conscious of the curious looks they were getting from their fellow passengers because of their matching attire.

'Do you think the whole weekend's going to be this frantic?' panted Phil as he handed in his ticket to the flight staff.

'Nah, mate,' replied Simon, 'Take it from me, my son, this is the easy part.'

4.

Having gratefully consumed (after much mockery) the packed lunch Helen had made within half an hour of taking off, the group spent the remainder of the journey trading drinking stories. They'd landed at Schiphol Airport, caught the express train into Amsterdam Centraal and were now standing in the square outside the station enjoying what Deano claimed to be the best sight so far: six beautiful twentysomething girls, all wavy hair, summer tops and short shorts, making the most of the early afternoon sun.

'Wherever they go tonight,' drooled Deano, 'is where I am going to be.'

'Mate,' said Simon, as the girls passed by oblivious of the boys' appreciative gaze, 'if they've got any sense they'll be spending the weekend in a different country not hanging around bars here waiting for you to pester them.'

Deano grinned. 'This kind of bitterness really doesn't become you, fella.'

'Bitter? Why should I be bitter?'

'Because you're married, mate. So tonight while I'm giving it the chat with some young Dutch filly, you will have no choice but to look and bite your fist in – that's right, I said it – *bitterness.*'

'Mate.' Simon put his arm around Deano and planted a patronising kiss on his friend's head. 'If I'm biting my fist while you're talking to some young Dutch filly it'll be for one reason only: to stop myself laughing as she kicks you to the kerb. Don't forget, I've seen you in action. Watching you on the pull is like watching a car crash in slo-mo. You want to look away but you just can't.'

The boys burst into raucous belly laughter, momentarily drawing the attention of the girls. Phil looked up at the perfect blue sky, closed his eyes and soaked up the sensation of the sun on his face. It was going to be a good weekend, a really good weekend.

'Fun though this is,' he said, 'we should get to the hotel, check in and start enjoying ourselves. This weather is too good to waste.'

'Phil's right,' said Spencer, 'the sooner we get to the hotel the sooner we can get the beers in.'

'And what about the suits?' asked Degsy tugging on the lapel of his jacket. He looked like an overgrown schoolboy on his way to a funeral. 'I don't know about you lot but I'm baking in this thing. Are we ditching them?'

'It's up to Phil,' said Simon. 'What do you reckon? Suits on or suits off?'

Phil reflected. However corny Simon's idea had been, as Spencer had put it when they had queued up to go through immigration, they 'looked the business'.

'Suits on,' said Phil. 'After all it's not every day you get to look like you're in a movie.'

'What my boy wants, my boy gets,' nodded Degsy. 'But if we are going to look like a bunch of tarts for the rest of the day then at least let's get a group shot while we still look half decent.'

Rooting around in his bag Degsy pulled out a digital camera, and catching the eye of a young woman passing by called her over and asked her to take a couple of pictures of the boys. Embarrassed but game for a laugh the woman agreed and so the boys mugged for the camera while she snapped away.

Leaning over Degsy's shoulders the boys reviewed the woman's handiwork and while comments ranged from 'We look like bank managers,' to 'this picture's so cool I'm going to get it blown up and hang it in my living room,' Phil opted to keep his thoughts to himself because the only thing he could think of as he took in the boys' grinning faces was how lucky he was to have such a great bunch of mates by his side.

The Royal Standard, was, as Spencer put it, 'a hotel with a two-star upstairs and four-star downstairs'. So while the lobby looked like London's Bloomsbury the rooms were more like Blackpool's Golden Mile. Disappointed though they were by the threadbare carpets and dated decor, this only served to reinforce their resolve to spend as much time out of the hotel as possible, so once they had dumped their bags they were back downstairs in the lobby ready to investigate all that Amsterdam had to offer.

Much as Phil hoped that there might be the

opportunity at some point of seeing Amsterdam's more cultural sights, he knew they wouldn't be going anywhere or doing anything before sinking the first pint of the weekend. With this in mind they headed to Leidseplein.

When Phil had told the guys at work where he was going for his stag weekend, Leidseplein had been the place they had all agreed that he should visit and as the boys finally reached their destination, having passed all manner of interesting bars and cafés on the way, Phil could see exactly why: it was a stag weekend paradise. A large square, surrounded on all sides by bars, cafés, restaurants and pubs and with more of the same on every street that radiated out from each corner, it was as if a team of Dutch town planners had consulted with a broad range of young British men in order to come up with their perfect weekend destination. Ticking all the boxes from all-you-can-eat curry houses within staggering distance of Irish theme pubs right through to industrial sized coffee houses with menus featuring twenty-two different kinds of hash, it was a veritable cornucopia of manly distractions and as such, pretty much the perfect location for the boys to have their first pint of the weekend.

Choosing a pub with outdoor seating overlooking the busy square, the boys sat down at an empty table, rearranged the chairs to accommodate their group and donned their sunglasses, certain, if only for this particular moment, that this was indeed the life.

A waitress approached. She was young and pretty

and it was a forgone conclusion that Deano would try and chat her up.

'Good afternoon, gentlemen,' she began with a smile. 'You look very hot in those suits.'

'We're working a look,' explained Deano, before anyone else could respond, 'you know, *Reservoir Dogs*. Quentin Tarantino. You must have seen it.'

She nodded and smiled knowingly. 'So you and your friends are on a British stag party? No?'

'We are as it happens,' he replied, 'but I have been here on business before now.'

'Which business is that, mate?' teased Phil. 'Banking? Finance? Novelty rubber chickens?'

'I'll have you know I have business dealings that might surprise you, thank you very much,' retorted Deano in a bid to save face. 'It's not just Si and Reuben who know a thing or two about the FTSE 100.'

'Mate,' laughed Simon. 'You know nothing about the Footsie one hundred. Don't forget I do your accounts. I've seen your way with a calculator and it's not nice.'

Confused, the waitress continued with her patter. 'So, are you liking Amsterdam so far?'

'We're liking it a lot more now you're here,' leered Deano.

As embarrassed for Deano as he was for the waitress, Phil stepped in. 'Any chance we could order a couple of lagers?'

'Yes, yes of course.' She took their orders and returned inside the bar.

Reuben groaned at Deano. 'Could you have been any more obvious about trying to get into her knickers?'

'I was doing no such thing!' protested Deano. 'I was merely making conversation. That's what human beings do.'

'She was barely eighteen! You dirty old perv!' chuckled Degsy. 'You're old enough to be her geography teacher!'

'Are you lot going to be like this the whole weekend?' sulked Deano. 'You're seriously cramping my style.'

'If this is you in action I can safely say that you won't need us to cramp your style, you're killing it as it is.'

Deano and Reuben's bickering seemed to set the tone for the rest of the afternoon, and as the ice-cold lagers arrived and the light-hearted banter continued, Phil thought their afternoon together was one of the best they had enjoyed for months. Everybody seemed on good form, the conversation as always veered between vaguely intelligent political debate and downright silliness, and the heat of the sun made everything perfect.

Some hours later as the afternoon gave way to early evening Phil made his way back to the table from what felt like his hundredth trip to the loo when it occurred to him that if he hadn't handed his phone over to Simon, about now would have been when he would have paused to send Helen a text telling her how well things were going. It felt odd not being able to undertake this small but important act and even more odd that he'd only now realised how important these daily interactions with Helen were to him. Some of his friends might interpret such a desire as an indication that he was under the thumb, but he wasn't all that bothered. Whether he was just about to be awarded the Nobel Peace Prize or had snagged a fingernail on his favourite jumper, there was one person in the world to whom the news would be equally important as it was to him.

As Phil approached the boys he sensed that something was wrong. When he had left they had been swapping anecdotes about their best holidays but now they were oddly muted, as though for his benefit they had hastily arranged a change of topic for which none of them could muster much enthusiasm.

His curiosity piqued, Phil determined to monitor the situation and so picked up his half empty beer glass while the conversation limped on around him like the work of a bunch of bad actors in an improv class.

'No, I can't stand them,' said Reuben.

'Me neither,' said Spencer.

'They're all right,' said Degsy. 'Mind, I have to be in the right mood for them like.'

There was a long silence then Deano looked at Simon. 'What about you mate?'

'They're not bad, I suppose,' shrugged Simon. 'But I can't say they'd make my top five.'

Phil could torture them no more. 'What's wrong with you lot?'

'What are you talking about?' said Degsy, delivering his outrage like a second-rate soap star. 'There's nothing wrong with us.'

'No? So why when I left you were all having a laugh and now I'm back you're talking about . . . let me guess . . . how you feel about cheese and onion crisps?' Degsy widened his eyes as though convinced his best mate had learned how to read minds. 'Mate, how long have I know you? Thirty-odd years? Do you really think I don't know that under pressure to drum up a change of conversation your stock question is: what's your least favourite crisp flavour? You've been asking people that since we were at primary school. What are you hiding?'

'Nothing.'

Phil rolled his eyes as Deano cast a withering glance in Degsy's direction.

'I told you not to do the crisp thing,' snapped Deano.

'Don't try and drop me in it,' protested Degsy. 'It's not like anyone else was saying anything.'

Deano set his glass down on the table and addressed Phil. 'Look, mate, we didn't mean anything by it but you're right, we were sort of talking about you.'

'Only because you brought it up,' replied Spencer.

'Doesn't really matter who said what,' said Phil. 'All I want to know is what you were saying.'

'We were debating why you're getting married,' revealed Deano reluctantly, 'because, come on mate, it's not like you need to, is it? You and your missus have been together ages. Why would you want to change things for no good reason?'

'I've got my own good reasons, thank you very much.'

'Of course you have,' said Deano. 'And we shouldn't have brought it up. We were out of order.'

'You're right,' said Phil. 'But now the topic's up for grabs why don't you tell us why you married Sheena.'

Deano and Sheena had met at a pound a shot night at a bar in the centre of Nottingham back when Deano had been in his mid-twenties. A fiery relationship from its consummation, it wasn't expected to last beyond a few months, let alone the four years that they managed to rack up together as cohabitees, then husband and wife.

'Because it was what she wanted,' said Deano.

'So you just went along with the idea?'

'Pretty much.'

'Not exactly the greatest endorsement for marriage I've ever heard,' said Phil stifling a grin.

Deano mulled the comment over. 'We weren't that sort of couple,' he said swirling the remains of his lager in his glass. 'Things were fun before, but if we're being truthful it was signing on the dotted line that did for us in the end.'

Phil raised an eyebrow. 'And you carrying on with one of the barmaids had nothing to do with it?'

'I've told you before: that was a symptom, not the cause. If she hadn't caught me I would have caught her if I'd tried hard enough.'

Phil turned to Reuben. Reuben and Alena had been together nearly eight years having met through old university friends of Reuben. The first time Reuben introduced Alena to the boys he warned them up front that she wasn't just beautiful but actually '*stunningly* beautiful' and not to give into the temptation to stare at her like a colony of rabbits caught in her headlights. Phil assumed that Reuben was exaggerating for effect and so when he finally did meet Alena he was mentally so ill prepared for a woman so stunning that all he could do for the entire conversation was mumble.

'What about you Reub?' asked Phil. 'You're married. You must have had a good reason.'

Reuben shrugged. 'You'd think so, given that the whole thing cost the best part of eighteen grand wouldn't you?'

'But I know you proposed because Alena told Helen the whole story the week after you told everyone. Or was that her idea too?'

'Look,' sighed Reuben, 'I don't regret it but if we're all being honest here then I have to say it wasn't my idea. Alena started going on about it after we'd been together two years and although I probably would have done it under my own steam at some point, the truth is she forced the issue.'

'Gun to head style?'

'More veiled threats. She's a drop dead gorgeous half-Russian girl with a degree in Economics who likes football and tiny underwear. If I hadn't proposed she would've moved to London and snagged the nearest millionaire banker the second she got off the train at King's Cross.'

Phil turned to Spencer. 'Come on mate, what about you? You and Emma were together ages. Surely you must have at least thought about giving the marriage thing a go?'

'Why do you think she's not around any more?'

'I thought it was because you didn't want kids?'

'It was . . . in part. But the whole thing was wrapped up in a lot of other stuff too: marriage, kids, where we were going to live. The more she went on about her vision of the future the more I realised it didn't look anything like mine.'

Reuben laughed. 'You have a vision of the future? You must be joking! How many times have you missed out on stuff because you never make up your mind until the last minute? Last year's Party in the Park, that holiday we all took in Ibiza, the last time the Rams played Forest . . . the list goes on and on.'

'I don't like to be hemmed in that's all. I like my freedom.'

'And now you've got all the freedom you could ever wish for.'

Degsy took a sip from his glass and then spoke up: 'I would have married my Leah like a shot,' he said, unprompted, of the woman who was the mother of his two kids. He and Leah had met at secondary school and been off and back on again more times than a light switch. Right now they were going through an off stage that would soon be celebrating its second anniversary.

'So why didn't you?'

'I asked tons of times but she wouldn't have me. Said I was too much of a liability.'

'Should have proved her wrong, mate,' said Spencer. 'Birds love that sort of thing.'

'I tried.'

'And what? You proved her right instead?'

Everyone around the table did the bloke wince – that

universally accepted visual shorthand for: 'That was a bit below the belt, mate.' Chastened, Spencer held his hands aloft in admission of his overstepping the line. 'You're right, sorry about that Degs, okay mate?'

Degsy nodded half-heartedly and drained his glass.

There was only Simon left to speak now. Phil thought briefly about Simon and Yaz's wedding day and the inside view that he had got of their relationship through his role as best man. If anyone had anything positive to say about marriage it would be Simon.

'So come on then, Si,' said Phil, 'Only you left to reveal all. Why did you and Yaz decide to get hitched?'

'Love,' said Simon after a long, ponderous silence.

Phil had had enough individual heart-to-heart conversations with the boys over the years to know that despite their bluster the boys were far from being emotional cripples but even he was a little shocked by his friend's frankness and unsure what to do to relieve the resulting tension. Phil could see his friends mulling over the various options available from a well timed fart gag through to the suggestion that they should all check out the arse on the waitress who was currently bending over to pick up a teaspoon that had fallen on the floor. In the end Phil himself provided the six friends with the best way out of the conversational cul-de-sac in which they found themselves.

'I'm starving,' said Phil. 'Who's hungry?'

'I am,' said Simon getting to his feet. Then he added, almost as if the news had only just occurred to him, 'Oh, and by the way I've left Yaz.'

5.

Phil knew Simon wanted everyone around the table to carry on as if nothing had happened because that was the way the friends had always chosen to deal with big news. Like the time Degsy told everyone that his girlfriend wouldn't let him see his kids any more. The time Reuben revealed that he and his wife were struggling to get pregnant. The time Deano confessed that his dad was dying of liver cancer. Each of these moments had been met with silence. A silence that acknowledged the scale and magnitude of the problem in question while recognising the pointlessness of any words the English language might offer in such a situation. The silence said without actually vocalising: 'I feel your pain, mate, feel free to fill in the blanks.'

Perhaps if this had been any other friend, Phil might have let him get away with dropping such a bombshell without cause for a soap opera style reaction and immediate dissection. But this wasn't any other friend, this was one of his oldest and closest friends. His best man. And they weren't in a dark corner of some shabby Beeston pub on a Tuesday night. They were sitting outside a bar in central Amsterdam, with the specific intention of celebrating Phil's last weekend as an unmarried man. Regardless of any accusations that might come his way following his failure to observe the rules of The Great Book of Bloke, Phil *was* going to ask questions. And lots of them. He just couldn't see any way around it.

'You've done what?'

Simon closed his eyes, making clear the extreme nature of his disappointment. A number of moments passed by then he opened them again and said: 'Look, I know it's a shock mate, but there's a time and place and this isn't it. I just thought you all ought to know.'

Still refusing to obey the rules of the game, Phil continued with his line of enquiry: 'How long?'

'A while,' replied Simon. 'Now let it go.'

Phil attempted to process this information but needed some kind of explanation.

'Why?'

Simon's half-embarrassed shrug appeared to acknowledge its own woeful inadequacy.

Phil felt like shaking some sense into his friend. He thought about Yaz and what might be going through her mind, because after all the years he had known her she was as much his friend as Helen's.

'How's Yaz taken it?'

'She's fine.' He looked down at the table and added: 'She'll probably tell Helen this weekend.'

Phil swallowed hard. He didn't like the idea of Helen getting this news so close to the wedding. He'd lost count of the number of times in the past that problems in the relationships of people *he didn't even know* had ruined his evenings by replacing an evening's DVD viewing with a three-hour debate about 'feelings'. If Yaz told Helen about her bust-up with Simon then it stood to reason the debate about 'feelings' would be longer than three hours. Much longer.

'What about the kids?'

'They're fine too.'

'Really?'

The muscles in Simon's jaw tensed. 'You need to stop now,' he said leaving out the words: 'or you and I are going to fall out', mainly because they were clearly implied. Simon had never been one for making empty threats. The others were slack-jawed watching the conversation unfold. No one knew what to do. No one said a word. A group of young Spaniards with designs on their table hovered in the corner of Phil's eye line.

Phil signalled to all the terms of his peace accord with Simon – unconditional surrender – and adopted his best non-judgemental face to look back at his friend. 'Still hungry?'

'Starving.'

'Right,' said Phil. 'Then let's go and get something to eat.'

In a bid to lighten the mood as they walked across the square and down a side street packed with restaurants, Degsy started a conversation about a documentary on the Discovery channel about the science behind how swords are forged. It focused on a guy in America who had honed the art to such a degree that he was now able to produce broadswords that could near enough slice a small tree in two.

Under normal circumstances Degsy would have been lucky to get so much as a grunt out of a conversational gambit of that calibre but there was little choice but to make the most of it.

As his friends, with the exception of Simon, began offering up a hitherto unsuspected depth of knowledge about broadsword production, Phil scanned the road ahead for a suitable restaurant while his mind was firmly on Simon.

It didn't make sense, Simon leaving Yaz like that. Simon and Yaz were one of the best-matched couples that he knew, with Yaz's stridency being tempered by Simon's own laid-back nature. There were half a dozen couples of his and Helen's acquaintance that he would have guessed more likely to split up than these friends. This really was a bolt from the blue.

His automatic assumption was that Simon had met somebody else possibly through work. But having met a number of his female colleagues Phil couldn't imagine which it might be. Maybe Yaz was at fault and not Simon at all, but although she frequently talked of running off with Jude Law, you only had to be around her when she'd had a glass of wine or two to see just how much she still fancied Simon after all these years.

Whatever the reason, it sounded as if it had been Simon's decision not Yaz's and, while he hoped that there was no one else involved, experience told him that this was unlikely. As Helen had said to him the evening that their friend Lou had announced that Hamish had walked out after eleven years together insisting that no one else was involved: 'When it comes to men leaving women there's always someone else. Always. Men don't leave wives and girlfriends to be on their own. It's just not how they work.'

So who was this woman? Phil considered his friend, his head bowed, and his face fixed in a surly demeanour, walking in silence just behind Spencer and Reuben. There was no clue to be had.

Having dismissed countless eateries for the flimsiest of reasons the boys found themselves at a junction and took a left while dodging past crowds of after-work drinkers, groups of exchange students and rival stag parties.

On a hunch, Phil had begun following a group of young revellers who looked like they knew where they were going when Degsy tugged his arm.

'What about this place?' he asked.

'You joking?' Phil eyed the Union Jack in the window of the Britannia Chippy.

'Never been more serious,' replied Degsy. 'I'm starving, mate, if we eat here we could be in and out and back on the beer in no time.'

'He's got a point,' said Reuben. 'I'm not really in the mood for anything too fancy.'

Phil looked at the rest of his friends. 'Anyone not want chips?' The boys' hands remained resolutely at their sides. Phil's spirits fell. At best he'd have settled for a Dutch restaurant so they could sample some typical local food and at worst he'd have settled for a curry in a restaurant that they had never been to before, but chips from a chip shop that could easily have been found on any high street back home disappointed him more than he wanted to let on.

Degsy ordered six portions of fish and chips and six cans of Coke and Simon paid for them out of a hastily arranged kitty while the rest of the boys spread themselves across two Formica tables.

The food was ready within minutes and to Phil's surprise was actually quite good, given that Degsy had discovered during the course of a long and involved conversation that the proprietor, a small, hirsute man who may or may not have been Greek, had never so much as set foot in England.

By the time they'd finished eating all thoughts of divorce and indeed broadswords had long since disappeared, and although they would have all scoffed at the idea there did seem to be a new enthusiasm, as though they had all decided that the evening needed rescuing and it was up to them to do it.

'We need to start drinking again,' said Reuben. 'This food has sobered me up no end.'

As one they all stood up and thanking the chip shop owner politely as they left, stepped out into the street.

'How about over there?' said Deano.

They followed his pointing finger across the road to a fashionable looking bar where a huge queue waited to go inside.

'Now you're talking,' said Degsy. 'Where there's a queue there's action!'

They joined the queue behind an impossibly handsome couple dressed in black who appeared to be more interested in the contents of their BlackBerries than they did in each other.

After ten minutes in the queue, and still feeling some residual distress at Simon's news, Phil was about to suggest to the boys that maybe they should try somewhere else, when the impossibly handsome couple simultaneously looked up from their phones, took in the number of people currently ahead of them and after murmuring to each other in Dutch, cast a withering glance in the boys' direction and left the queue.

'Maybe we should join them,' said Reuben closing the gap so that they were now behind a group of well dressed women. 'By the looks of the trendy types in this queue there's every chance we won't get in even if we do make it to the front before midnight and to top it all we don't even know what we're queuing for. It could be Amsterdam's top gay bar for all we know.'

'And even then you wouldn't be able to pull!' said Deano dodging past Phil and tapping one of the women in front of them on the shoulder.

The woman turned round and Phil was surprised at how attractive she was. She had black shoulder-length hair and a luminous complexion that made her look fresh and youthful. She looked like she was an actress or a model or even a singer and because of this Phil began to imagine that he recognised her.

'Can I help you?' she asked in English. Her accent although clearly European, was very MTV American.

'Yes, you can,' said Deano ditching his Derby accent for his best Hugh Grant 'yes-I-am-that-unbelievably-English' impression. Phil could barely keep a straight face. 'My friends and I were wondering if there was any chance you could tell us what this place is. It's just that we haven't a clue but thought it might be fun.' He looked up at the sign above their heads. 'The Lab. What is it?'

Phil cringed. This poor woman had done nothing to deserve the full Deano onslaught but now that his friend had started there was little chance that he would stop until expressly told to do so. Possibly by the police.

'It's just a bar,' said the beautiful woman. 'It opened a week or two ago and you know how it is when something's cool . . . everyone has to be there. It's my first time. I'm here for my friend's birthday.'

'But it'll be worth the wait?'

The beautiful woman laughed. 'Well, I'm hoping it'll beat sitting in front of the TV.' She turned back to her friends, leaving Deano staring lasciviously at her bare shoulders. Phil tapped him on the arm thereby ending what was clearly a sordid reverie.

'We should go,' said Phil, keen to stay as far away as possible from women who weren't his fiancée.

'Can't,' said Deano. 'First, Simon doesn't want to leave, do you Si?' Simon laughed and rolled his eyes. 'And second, I think I may possibly be in love.'

'This *is* still my stag do isn't it?' said Phil exasperatedly. 'I do still get some say in what we do?'

'Of course you do,' said Deano. 'Just not yet. You know how it is mate.' He lowered his voice. 'I have to talk to this woman again. She was well into me. And her mates are hot too!'

There wasn't enough alcohol in the entire world to make either this woman or her friends remotely interested in Deano but this made not one jot of difference to his friend.

'Fine, we'll stay,' said Phil reasoning that Deano's antics would offer some much needed light relief. 'But I'm nobody's wingman all right? I don't want to talk to, look at, or stand next to any of these women okay?'

'Ha!' scoffed Deano. 'Like they'd even be looking in your direction!'

Before Phil could reply to Deano's insult with a few of his own, his attention was caught by a group of four lads swaggering down the street towards them. From their accents, demeanour and general lack of sobriety it was obvious that they were part of a British stag party.

They came to a halt next to the beautiful woman and her friends. 'All right girls?' said the tallest of the men in a rough Essex accent. 'What's this queue for then?'

In an attempt to humour them, the beautiful woman explained very carefully what the queue was for but if they hoped that this would be enough to make the stag party go away they couldn't have been more wrong. Without any encouragement the men attempted to join the women in the queue and when they made it clear that they didn't want to be joined things began to get ugly.

'Stuck up bitches aren't interested, boys!' said the tall man to his friends. 'British blokes not good enough for you lot?'

'Not in this case,' said the beautiful woman. 'So why don't you just leave us alone?'

'You heard her,' said Phil, embarrassed by his fellow countrymen. He stepped in front of the beautiful woman so that he was facing the tall guy head on. 'They're not interested.'

Tall Guy glared at Phil. 'And you are?'

'Someone who's sick and tired of brain-dead morons like you giving us all a bad name.'

Tall Guy laughed. 'Boys, this cock in a suit thinks he can tells us what to do!'

'He does because he can,' said Simon positioning himself next to Phil, flanked by the rest of the boys. 'You, my friend, need to go, and you need to go now.'

Phil could see Tall Guy's friends weighing up the odds, but drunk as they were, they could see they were outnumbered – and thanks to Reuben and in particular Spencer – out-bulked too.

'Come on lads,' said Tall Guy fixing Phil with a menacing stare. 'One way or another I'm sure we'll see these guys around later.'

Wary of being caught off guard, the boys stood their ground as the Essex stag party sauntered into the mid-distance, and only once they were sure they had gone did they relax.

'He's right you know,' said Phil. 'Chances are we will see them later. It's not like Amsterdam is a huge place.'

'And when we do,' replied Simon, 'we'll sort them out just like we did this time.'

Phil turned to the beautiful woman. 'You all right?'

She nodded. 'Thank you for that. You were really kind to help out.'

'It was nothing,' replied Phil, suddenly self-conscious. 'I hope that it doesn't spoil your evening.'

Content to relive every nanosecond of their altercation (an event that quickly became known as The Time We Kicked Arse While Wearing Reservoir Dogs Suits) the next twenty minutes passed by in a blur of posing and posturing. Just as even Deano was beginning to murmur that maybe they had spent too long in the queue, a large group left the bar and the door staff began letting people in again and in no time at all the boys were second in the queue.

Readying themselves for their first encounter with Dutch door staff the boys tried to make themselves as presentable as they could fixing ties and sorting out collars. One of the bouncers, a tall wide-neck manmountain lifted the rope at the front of the entrance and then addressed the women: *'Zijn deze jongens met jou?'*

Phil breathed a sigh of relief. Despite their suits the doorman had seen the boys for exactly what they were: six British blokes on a stag do – the very epitome of the kind of customer any half-decent Dutch drinking establishment would not want to entertain for the evening. Soon they would be turned away and left with no choice but to find themselves a proper pub where they could drink, argue and talk nonsense without cause to contemplate the opposite sex.

But then the beautiful woman turned, winked at Phil and without missing a beat said in English: 'Yes, they are.'

6.

Phil had no idea what to think but as the doorman ushered the boys inside he reasoned that at the very least they would soon be getting a drink. A combination of the chips, the queuing and their near fight had sobered him up and he was now desperate to get back to that easy-going state of mind that he'd enjoyed earlier in the evening.

Inside, Phil made sure not to be too close to the women ahead in case they feared that he was going to spend all night following them and making a nuisance of himself following his good deed. Once they were past the second set of doors, however, the women peeled off to the right and joined a group at a table opposite the huge plate glass windows that looked out on to the street and Phil made sure to go the opposite way.

As the boys gathered Phil glanced over at the woman and she looked up at him and smiled. Phil smiled back and to show his appreciation of her kindness in a non-threatening manner devoid of all sexual connotations gave her the thumbs-up and immediately regretted it.

'I just gave that girl who got us in here the thumbs-up,'

shouted Phil over the bar's club music, as the woman looked on confused.

'We know,' yelled Deano, lines of laughter apparent at the corner of his eyes. 'We saw. After that public display of eighties-style sign language I think you've pretty much ruined all our chances. You gave her the wacky thumbs-up, fella! Even with the best will in the world there's no coming back from that mate. Beer?'

Phil nodded. 'I'll have whatever they've got. Just make sure it's cold and strong.'

Led by Simon, the boys headed off to get the drinks leaving Phil alone with Deano. Phil had been to many bars like The Lab in his time and he had loathed every aspect of them from their pretentious decor through to their even more pretentious clientele. These weren't so much places to have a drink and a catch up with mates but rather places that people went to in order to see and be seen, as though the very act of having made it past the door staff made you something special.

Phil did not feel special. In fact having compromised his beliefs by coming here he felt sort of dirty and soiled and wished he could be in their usual corner in Deano's pub back in Beeston, sipping Carlsberg while cracking jokes about Degsy's love life.

'What are we doing here?' asked Phil as a couple of attractive women passed by looking straight through them. 'This isn't us. After this beer we should go, find ourselves a proper pub and bed in for the night.' He scanned the bar. All the seats had long since been taken and even standing room was at a premium. 'There isn't even anywhere to sit.'

'Mate,' said Deano, 'are you ever going to stop bloody moaning? All you've done all evening is whinge. Look around you, fella, this place is crawling with top class talent of every description!' He pointed to a tall girl with shoulder-length blonde hair. 'She's gorgeous!' He moved his finger across to the right by several degrees to a beautiful girl wearing a silver metallic barely there minidress. 'What I wouldn't do to be able to lick her armpits!' And finally he moved his finger to a beautiful brunette who was now looking right at him. 'Look at her! She's lovely! And because she's seen me pointing at her I'm on her radar!'

'As a potential stalker!' said Phil marvelling at his friend's brazenness. 'She's probably calling the police as we speak.'

A group of people at a table a few feet away stood up and left but before Phil could make a grab for their seats they were leapt upon by a group of young guys in tight tops sporting inordinate amounts of gel in their hair.

Thwarted, Phil turned to Deano and tried to make conversation to distract himself from the pain in his knees. 'So what's your take on this business with Si? It doesn't sound right does it?'

'Not even a little bit. It's got to be another bird though.'

'Any ideas who?'

Deano shrugged. 'I've seen him chat to a few women

in the pub but no more than a quick hello. But that's Si, isn't it? He'll talk to anyone about anything when he's on form. I didn't even notice he'd stopped wearing his wedding ring.'

'Has he? I didn't even think to look.'

'I clocked it when he told us in the bar.' Deano paused. 'You're not going to let it bother you though? You know, let it get under your skin, and convince you that all marriages are doomed and blah, blah, blah.'

Phil laughed. 'I hadn't been thinking that but cheers for putting it out there fella.'

'I'm just saying . . .'

'What?'

'Nothing.'

'What?'

'Nothing.'

'Are we going to carry on like this all night?'

Deano sighed. 'All I was going to say is that I've seen you and Helen together and I can tell – just from looking at you guys – that you're going to work.'

There was an awkward pause then Phil said: 'Was that as hard to say as it was to listen to?'

'Mate,' replied Deano, 'it was excruciating.'

'Let's agree to never do that again, okay?'

'On that,' said Deano, 'you have my absolute word.'

Although The Lab turned out to be more fun than he expected (even as a happily engaged man it was hard to not be impressed by the high concentration of gorgeous girls in the bar), after an hour or so there was no getting away from the fact that the lager was too expensive, there still weren't any seats and although Deano had toned down his dog on heat routine there was still every chance that the evening would end with the boyfriend of one of his victims punching his lights out.

Returning from a trip to The Lab's toilets (not so much your common or garden toilet as state of the art unisex space pod featuring toilets, with male and female urinals) Phil began working his way back to the boys trying to work out exactly how best to pitch his plan without getting into an hour long debate about the pros and cons of moving on. To his immediate discomfort he saw the woman from the queue standing in front of him.

'Ah, Mr Thumbs-up!' she grinned. 'We meet again.'

Phil cringed but as he tried to compose himself he was once again struck by the familiarity of her face. He couldn't possibly know her, could he? Surely she was far too attractive for him to have met her in person and forgotten.

'Look,' said Phil. 'I am very much aware how uncool that thumbs-up thing was.'

'I thought it was funny. Quite sweet actually. Sometimes I miss the English and their funny ways.'

'You know England then?'

'A bit. I'm actually half English. My dad was a Londoner but I was raised here in Amsterdam, then moved to London in my twenties. I haven't been to the UK for a while but if there's one thing I miss about the English, it's the way that you moan. No one, not even the Danes, can moan like you Brits. It's your nation's most endearing feature.'

'Yeah, well,' said Phil. 'We do begrudgingly aim to please.'

Phil thought this had better be the end of the conversation. 'Well,' he said. 'It was nice to meet you.'

'You too,' she replied. 'And I really want to thank you for your assistance outside. I hope the rest of your stag weekend goes well. Congratulations. I hope marriage suits you better than it did me.'

Phil eyed the woman suspiciously. 'How did you know I was the one getting married? Do I look engaged?'

'It's in your eyes, I think,' she said. 'But it's not a bad thing. It's nice. Believe me you don't want to be like that friend of yours.'

'Deano? He's not that bad. You know what they say about barks being worse than bites? Well that's him all over.'

'Maybe. But I stand by what I said. You don't want to be like him.'

'I'll try not to be.'

'So what's planned for the rest of your boys' weekend? Anything good? No fights I hope.'

'Oh, no . . .' said Phil. 'We'll probably just be doing the usual stuff.'

'Visiting the red-light area, getting stoned and drinking 'til you throw up?'

'I thought you said you liked the Brits?' protested Phil. 'We're not all clichés.'

'So tomorrow you and the guys will be hitting Amsterdam's top cultural spots? Stedelijk followed by the Van Gogh Museum then after lunch heading to

Oude Kerk and maybe finishing the day off at the Begijnhof?'

'We might be.'

The woman clearly wasn't convinced. 'Now that,' she said, 'I'd love to see.'

'Does it get you down?' asked Phil moving out of the way of a couple trying to get around him. 'Having your country invaded every weekend by hordes of Brits?'

She shook her head. 'Not really. I don't go out that often. I just sometimes wish you lot would recognise there's more to Amsterdam than clogs, hash and working girls.'

'In that case,' said Phil raising his right hand. 'In return for getting us in here tonight – thanks for that by the way – I hereby promise to go somewhere cultural tomorrow. You name it and I'll go there.'

'Seriously?'

Phil grinned. 'I never joke about culture.'

'Then in that case you should go to the Van Gogh Museum. It's nice there. Plenty to see. You'll love it.'

Phil smiled as if to say, 'Well I suppose that's that,' and she offered him a smile in return. Carefully wrapping his thumbs inside his fists in case they got ideas of their own he headed back to his friends.

'Where have you been?' said Reuben. 'We were about to send out a search party!'

'Nowhere,' said Phil rolling over the encounter in his mind. 'I just got a bit lost that's all. This place is bigger than you think.' He took his glass from Degsy and drained it in one. 'I was thinking that maybe we should get off?'

'No can do, mate,' said Deano.

'Why not?'

Deano looked over Phil's shoulder. 'Because I think the woman of my dreams has finally come to her senses.'

Phil turned around to see the woman from the queue walking over to them. 'For you,' she said, handing him a torn piece of paper, 'to thank you for your help earlier and in case you use not having anyone to go with as an excuse to chicken out.'

Phil looked at the paper in his hand. A name and mobile number written in the same gloriously feminine handwriting.

'Cheers . . .' he looked down again, 'Sanne . . . that's really nice of you.'

'You're welcome,' she replied, nodded a brief acknowledgement to the boys and headed back to her friends leaving him with five pairs of eyes staring at him.

'What was that about?' asked Deano.

'Nothing,' said Phil. 'I bumped into her a few minutes ago. We were just talking, that's all.'

'And now she's giving you her phone number?'

Phil nodded.

'And you think this is normal?'

He hesitated. 'Maybe not normal exactly but . . .' His voice trailed off. 'Look, I just bumped into her, that's all. We started talking about museums and stuff and

I'd said I'd check one of them out and that's why she gave me her number, okay? Nothing sinister . . . she's simply offering to go with me if I want her to.'

'And do you?'

'No, of course not.'

'Then give it to me,' said Deano making a grab for the paper.

'It wasn't like that, okay?' said Phil snatching it away. 'She knows I'm getting married.'

'You told her?'

'She guessed and I saw no reason to deny it.'

Deano shrugged as though this made no difference to his overall judgement of the situation. 'So are you going to call her or not?'

'What with? My phone's in England.'

Deano rolled his eyes. 'Mate, guess what? It's just like home. They have payphones.'

Phil shook his head. 'No,' he said firmly. 'I will not be calling her. Even though she was simply being nice and I'm sure there was nothing in it I think it's probably best if I don't.'

The boys jeered.

'She wasn't being nice,' said Spencer. 'She was after a slice of Hud pie! Girls used to go mental for your sensitive guy schtick back in the day. Do you remember that one with the legs up to her armpits at that campsite in the south of France? How long did she write to you for?'

Phil groaned. Sometimes he wished he'd never taken that holiday. 'Nearly a year.'

'And you wouldn't let her come over!'

'She had a boyfriend.'

'Once again you miss the point. Who cares? She was loads hotter than the girls we were knocking around with back then.'

'Can we stop this?'

'We're only just getting started!'

Phil gave Deano a threatening look not altogether dissimilar from the one Simon had given him when he too had overstepped the mark.

'Fine,' said Deano relenting. 'Have it your way. We should probably get going anyway. I read on the web about some bar near the red-light district staffed completely by eastern European girls wearing nothing but thongs.'

Phil didn't even comment. He just threw Deano a glance that said: 'Over my dead body.'

'A mate of mine told me about a place off Dam Square that does speciality beers,' said Spencer. 'You know the type, high alcohol, knock your head off stuff. What do you reckon?'

'Sounds a bit tame if you ask me,' said Deano.

Simon laughed. 'What are you after? A dwarf only bondage bar? Mate, it's not even midnight yet. Calm down.'

The boys finished their drinks and proceeded towards the exit of the bar. Phil threw a last glance back in the direction of Sanne and her friends. Completely oblivious to him she was deep in conversation.

'Are you coming or what?'

Reuben was holding the door open for him.

Shaking his head free of thoughts he didn't want there Phil nodded and left the bar.

It was still just light outside. Spencer got out the map from the hotel, checked their position and pointed in the direction that they needed to go.

They had only been walking a few minutes when Phil turned to Spencer and asked: 'Did she look familiar to you? You know the girl that gave me her number.'

'Not really. Why should she have done?'

'Now you mention it,' said Simon overhearing the conversation. 'You might have a point. Her face . . . it is sort of familiar. What was her name again?'

'Sanne.'

Simon shook his head. 'You'd remember a name like that wouldn't you? I don't know any Sannes do you?'

'That's the thing,' said Phil. 'Even the name sounds familiar.'

'What do you think she is?' asked Spencer. 'An actress or a model? She's good-looking enough to be both.'

'I'm pretty sure it's something like that,' said Phil, dodging past a couple of drunken English guys sitting on the kerb. 'If I had my phone with me I could have Googled her.'

'If you'd had your phone with you, Deano would have nicked it and spent the night posting libellous status updates on your Facebook page,' chipped in Reuben.

'Hang on,' said Degsy, clearly not wanting to be left out of the conversation, 'wasn't there a girl called Sanne in that girl band that had a couple of hits a few years back? I only know that because my eldest was mad about them for a while. What was their name again? Misty something or other . . .'

'Misty Mondays!' shouted Phil. 'That was it! She was the—' Phil stopped. He knew exactly who she was and why he recognised her. 'This is absolutely the weirdest thing,' he began, 'but I've remembered how I know her and it's not just the band thing either.' He looked at Degsy. 'She used to be married to . . . Aiden Reid.'

'The radio DJ?'

Phil nodded.

'Really?' mused Degsy, 'I know a lot of people think he's a tosser because he's loaded and always copping off with top models but I have to say I love his show. Funniest thing in the world. That thing he does with his co-host Crazy Dave cracks me up every time.' He stopped and looked at Phil. 'I suppose it is a bit weird that you've been chatted up by Aiden Reid's ex-missus. Maybe you could sell the story to the tabloids: "Radio Star's Ex Gives Bloke From Nottingham Her Number".'

'You're not getting it,' said Phil. 'That's not even the weird part. The weird part is that Aiden Reid is the last bloke that Helen went out with before she met me.'

'Really?'

'Yeah, really.' What Phil neglected to add was that Aiden Reid was also the reason why after nine years together he and Helen had finally decided to get married.

Saturday

7.

As Phil made the transition from oblivion to consciousness he became aware that all was not well with his world. His temples throbbed as if his brain was trapped in a cycle of inflation and deflation: one moment taut and hard, pressing on to the outreaches of his skull and the next soft and saggy and barely taking up space in the cavernous void in which it was housed. The one constant in this situation was the pain, the deep, dull ache that in tempo and persistence seemed perfectly to echo the pace of his slow, dull pulse.

He was never going to drink again. Never. He would never go to the pub, visit a bar or even walk down the booze aisle of his local Morrison's. Drink was evil. He knew that now. After twenty-odd years of being legally able to indulge in the demon drink the lesson had finally been learned, the hard way. Now, all he needed to do was to survive the war of attrition between his body and the alcohol he had so willingly imbibed, and the booze free vision of the future that he had so keenly constructed would be his.

Lying very still, not even daring to move so much as a single muscle Phil built up the courage to open his eyes. Beginning a countdown from ten he fought against his instinct to preserve his cerebral cortex from yet more needless pain, and reaching zero prepared to open his eyes when something happened that made him squeeze his eyes shut tighter than ever: a foot of which he had no ownership grazed his lower calf. Phil's eyes shot open and he found himself looking directly into a face.

'Degsy!'

Degsy woke with a shock, mumbling incoherently. 'What are you shouting for?' he asked, mole-like eyes blinking.

'What do you mean what am I shouting for?' barked Phil. 'You're in my bed!'

'What's with all the bloody yelling?' called a voice from the other side of the room.

Phil looked at Degsy in confusion and flicked the switch on the wall by the bed. A dim pool of light illuminated a corner of the room. Phil could just about make out the outline of a body lying on the floor. Degsy picked up his pillow, crawled to the end of the bed and brought the pillow down sharply on the figure below. It yelled in surprise.

'That'll be Reuben,' said Degsy. 'I'd recognise that girly scream anywhere.'

Reuben, looking like death warmed up, sat up and scowled. 'Have you any idea what kind of headache I've got?'

'No,' said Degsy. 'But I promise you it's not a patch on mine.'

Phil looked from Reuben to Degsy and back again and noted that they were still wearing their suits and ties. He looked underneath the duvet and noted that he too was fully clothed.

Phil reached for the main light switch and as he flicked it on, the rest of the room came to life: Deano began unfurling from the foetal position from his place by the door, Spencer, still half asleep, twitched on Degsy's side of the bed, and scratching his head, Simon emerged from the darkness of the bathroom.

Speechless, Phil was fumbling for an explanation of the situation when out of the corner of his eye he noticed a red cement-splattered pneumatic drill leaning against the wall and a bright yellow hard hat crowning the TV.

Phil nudged Degsy with his elbow and silently pointed at them.

'Building site next to the hotel,' he said, through helpless laughter.

'You nicked them?' gasped Phil. 'Why?'

Degsy shrugged, 'I dunno, mate, why do men do anything? My memory's blitzed when it comes to motivation.'

'And where was I when all this was happening?'

'Asleep,' said Degsy. 'On a bench. You were out like a light, mate. We practically had to carry you back here. What was up with you last night? One minute you were you and the next it was like a night out with your old man.'

'It's true,' said Reuben, sitting down on the edge of the bed. 'Once we reached that place that sold the oddball beers you were like a man possessed. Honestly mate, by the end of the night you were so off your face we nearly got chucked out of the lap dancing club.'

Phil blinked hard. 'We went to a lap dancing club?'

'Not one,' explained Degsy. 'Two, one after the other. And then a strip bar and before you start complaining we didn't drag you anywhere. You dragged us. You said it was your stag do so you should get to choose.' Degsy squinted in Phil's direction. 'Don't you remember any of it?'

Phil shook his head and regretted it instantly. 'Not a second.'

'So what's the last thing that you actually do remember?'

Lying down on his pillow Phil closed his eyes as the major turning point of the evening – the woman from the queue being Aiden Reid's ex-wife – came back to him.

Unlike most boyfriends who for reasons of self-preservation jettison such information as soon as it's handed to them, Phil could recall perfectly the exact moment that Aiden Reid's name was first mentioned to him. It had been eight years earlier, he and Helen had been dating for about a year and they had been sitting in their local Thai takeaway waiting for a set meal for two when Phil had picked up a two-day-old copy of the *Sun* and begun reading an article entitled: 'Who will get top DJ job?'

The story was a follow-on from the biggest story of the previous week: the news that BBC breakfast radio DJ Xan Collins had been caught on film by the *News of the World* snorting cocaine in a hotel bedroom in Mayfair with two underage models. Despite Collins' record-breaking audience figures the BBC had had no option at all but to sack him on the spot, thereby creating a vacancy for the single most coveted job in the whole of UK radio, and the article was all about who should replace him.

Phil had been about to turn the page when Helen had pointed to the picture of one of the three DJs vying for the job, a ridiculously good-looking stubbly chinned type who he recognised from TV. 'That's my ex,' she said succinctly.

Phil was momentarily speechless. 'The one you were going to marry?'

Helen nodded and Phil stared at the paper. 'Your ex is Aiden Reid? Why didn't I know this before?'

'Why would you?' replied Helen. 'It's not like I know the names of all your exes, do I? I just thought I ought to say, that's all. Chances are, he's going to get that job, and if he does it's a guarantee that the tabloids will come sniffing around looking for a story on him. If they do, say nothing, not a single word. Not even in my defence.'

Helen was right. Not only about Aiden getting the BBC Radio breakfast job but also the tabloid hacks making contact, looking for a story about 'Aiden Reid's first love.' They called Helen constantly both at home and at work and when that failed to give them what they wanted they concentrated their efforts on Phil. 'How does it feel to be dating the ex of one of the country's most famous celebs, Mr Hudson? Anything you'd like to tell us about the way he went about wrecking your partner's life when they were engaged? We've got someone on record claiming that Aidan was the love of her life and that she's never got over him: would you care to comment?' Just as Helen had told him, Phil made no comment, but it was difficult, especially the lies about her never having got over him.

Running parallel to these events was Phil and Helen's relationship, which in a short space of time progressed from its tentative initial stages into something neither party had expected at all. Phil had never before experienced anything close to what he felt for Helen with anyone else and on the day that this had first dawned on him (a Sunday evening a year or so after the Aiden Reid furore) she was loading her car in order to drive back to Liverpool.

'We should get married,' said Phil as the thought occurred to him. Confused, Helen had stared at him blankly. 'I mean it,' he continued. 'I think we should get hitched.'

Helen didn't drive back to Liverpool that night. Instead she and Phil had stayed up until late with her explaining why although she felt as strongly for him as he did for her it was too soon to talk of marriage. Despite his enthusiasm Phil eventually came around to Helen's point of view, which is why he waited another year (by which time they were living together in Nottingham) to ask her for a second time as they celebrated their third anniversary of their first official date.

'I want you to marry me,' he said as they stood underneath the awning outside their favourite Italian restaurant on Weekday Cross sheltering from the rain as they waited for a cab home. 'I mean it, Helen, I'm absolutely convinced you're the one.'

Again Helen turned him down, citing a million and one reasons, from the fact that they were both very busy at work right through to the fact that they were looking to move to a bigger house soon and could do without the stress. Though clearly disappointed not to have received the yes he had been hoping for, Phil had eventually agreed, and so, having put the idea on the proverbial back burner, they both got on with the business of carving out a life for themselves.

But when Phil popped the question once again some two years later only to be met once again by the most logical of excuses, he made the decision that his days of proposing marriage were over for good. After all, enough was enough wasn't it? But then a few years later, following a date to the cinema and the finding of a child's toy plastic ring, not only was he back to proposing but after all these years and all these rejections he finally said out loud the one thing he hadn't dared to say all these years: that the reason Helen wouldn't marry him had nothing to do with him and everything to do with Aiden Reid.

The accusation not only hit home, but it hit home hard, so hard in fact that once he'd delivered a heartfelt declaration never to propose to Helen again, without missing a beat she actually proposed to him. And they were happy, really happy, or at least he'd thought so at the time. But now, as he lay in bed fighting through his raging hangover and reviewing his reaction to the news that Helen's ex had reared up in his life again, he began to wonder not only whether he was happy, but also if Helen, whom he had effectively bullied into saying yes, was happy too.

Leaving Phil to his thoughts the boys gathered themselves together and came up with a plan for the morning ahead.

'Well,' said Simon, 'I did have us down for something later in the day but that was before we got trashed, rolled in at five in the morning and kipped on the floor. Perhaps I'd better cancel it.'

Phil sat up. 'Don't,' he said firmly. 'Whatever it is let's do it anyway. Keep ourselves busy.'

Surprised by Phil's response, Simon shrugged: 'Fine, I'll leave it. But first off we've got to eat. How about we meet downstairs in half an hour, then nip out and find somewhere to get a decent breakfast.'

The boys began trooping out when a question occurred to Phil. 'I get the fact that things went a bit mental last night but what I don't understand is how you all came to be sleeping in my room.'

Degsy laughed. 'Who knows? I'm just glad that we didn't end up kipping in the hotel corridor like we did for my thirtieth. My back's never been the same.'

Alone in his room Phil yawned and ran a hand over his scalp hoping to calm the raging chaos inside his skull and then, summoning every last particle of his energy reserves, he made his way to the bathroom, turned on the light and as the extractor fan began whirring in the background stood looking at his reflection in the mirror above the sink.

Phil was perversely pleased to see that he looked as awful as he felt because he knew it would help make the case that he ought to stay sober for the rest of the weekend. Simon and Degsy were expert at drinking their way through the pain of even the worst hangovers and he knew that they would encourage the others to do the same. The prospect made Phil's stomach churn. He didn't want to get in that state ever again, even more so, having made the connection between his readiness to drink and the appearance (albeit in an abstract manner) of the man who had been a constant bone of contention in his relationship with Helen.

Reaching into his trouser pocket Phil pulled out Sanne's phone number. There was no way he would use it. Even though he had made it clear that he was getting married, she was an attractive woman and he, being a man, was programmed to find attractive women attractive. It really was a complication he could do without. He put it back in his pocket.

On the other hand, Sanne was Aiden Reid's ex-wife and having never met the man who had blighted his girlfriend's life to such an extent that she wouldn't even contemplate marriage the best part of a decade later, Phil was sorely tempted to meet her again, if only to find out what about Aiden (apart from his fame, good looks and bags of money) made him so special.

Phil knew it was a stupid, petty and childish way for a grown man to think, and that it was beneath him even momentarily to indulge these feelings of inadequacy. But in this instance at least what he felt in his heart carried more weight than what he thought in his rational mind.

Phil shed his suit, climbed into the bath, pulled back the curtain and turned on the shower, cowering away from the cool spray until steam began to rise from the lower reaches of the bath. Stepping under the hot water Phil's skin tingled as the water blasted through the dirt and grime that had plastered itself to him over the past twenty-four hours leaving him if not entirely like a different person, then at least the next best thing.

Stepping out of the bath he stood in front of the mirror, picked up his towel and wiped a patch of the glass free of condensation to reconsider his image. He looked better. Not great, but better. The eyes were less bloodshot, the sheen had returned to his skin and although his teeth were in need of a good sandblasting, it was nothing that a burst of Colgate and a good scrub couldn't handle.

In the bedroom Phil pulled out underwear and fresh clothes and then recalled his instruction that they should wear the suits for the entire weekend. He picked up his from the floor and hoped the worst of the creases would fall out during the day. The white shirt however was beyond redemption, so he pulled out another one and began dressing.

He put on his jacket and again fished out the piece of paper with Sanne's number on it. He stared at it a moment before screwing it up and tossing it on the table next to the TV. Congratulating himself on doing the right thing he picked up his room key and left the room, only to return, walk over to the pneumatic drill and hide it carefully in the wardrobe.

Reaching the ground floor Phil stepped out of the lift feeling more centred than he had any right to be given his hangover. And as he made his way to the lobby to meet the boys he promised himself that no matter what problems came his way during the day he would remain positive. There was no need to keep blowing up over the smallest thing, what he needed to do was to remain calm. As he scanned the lobby he spotted a scruffy denim-clad figure with a rucksack standing with friends. In an instant all notions of peace and goodwill to the universe vanished.

The man turned around and opened his arms to greet Phil. 'How's this for a surprise?' he said in a rich, deep voice like an old delta blues singer. He flashed Phil a dirty great grin that revealed a set of teeth which had seen better days. 'I bet you weren't expecting to see me here, were you, kid?'

'No, Dad,' said Phil flatly. 'You've pretty much hit the nail on the head with that one.'

8.

'Someone needs to explain!' barked Phil loudly enough for a number of the Royal Standard's guests to glance over at him. 'And they need to do it now!'

Simon stepped forward wearing a look of weary resignation. 'Well in that case I think it probably ought to be me.'

'You?' questioned Phil. 'You're supposed to be my best man not a cut-price Jeremy Kyle!'

Simon pulled Phil to one side and lowering his voice to a whisper said: 'Look, mate. Don't do this.'

'Do what?' boomed Phil, refusing to comply with the volume established by Simon. 'You're the one who invited my dad, of all people, on my stag do. What were you thinking?'

'He asked to come. What could I say?'

'I think no would have sufficed. That's the word you use when you don't want things to happen isn't it?' Fizzing with frustration Phil snarled: 'You didn't even bother to warn me!'

'Would you have still come if I had?'

'Of course I wouldn't! Why would I go on a stag do with my dad?'

'Because he's a laugh. He always has been.'

'He's only a laugh if you're not related to him. If you share DNA with the old scrote I think you'll find that the word "laugh" is better translated "embarrassment".'

'So what do you want me to do? Send him back?'

'Could you?' retorted Phil. 'That would be great! And while you're at it you could get him to pop round to my mum's and apologise to her for being an arsehole for the best part of forty years!' Phil glared at Simon. 'Did you pay his plane fare?'

Simon winced. 'He promised he'd pay me back.'

'What with,' snorted Phil, 'fresh air?'

They both turned to look at Patrick who already appeared to have the boys in stitches.

'So can he stay or what?' asked Simon.

'Doesn't look like I've got much choice, have I?' replied Phil bitterly. 'I'll tell you what though . . . next time you've got a big Saturday night blow-out planned I'm definitely bringing your mum along.'

Leaving Simon to contemplate the error of his ways Phil strode over to his dad and considered giving him a hug but thought better of it. He looked older, more worn than he remembered and it occurred to Phil that Patrick Hudson would not always be around to be angry at.

'So, all sorted then?' said Patrick raising his bushy eyebrows expectantly.

Phil nodded. 'It's done. You're staying.'

'Excellent, son!' he said genuinely pleased. 'I promise you, you won't regret it! So what's the plan? Bit too early to start drinking, eh? Especially after last night!' He nudged Phil in the ribs and ran one of his big calloused hands over his son's scalp. 'A right chip off the old block!'

'Cheers, Dad,' said Phil envisaging the long day ahead. 'You have no idea how proud that makes me feel.'

'We're going to get some breakfast, Mr Hudson,' said Simon.

Patrick eyed Simon sternly. 'It's Patrick, son. I'm only Mr Hudson when I'm in court or being grilled by the filth.'

Phil reluctantly found himself warming to his dad's infectious charm. 'Let it go Pop, it's not like you're the Godfather is it?' he said. 'The only criminal record you've got is for refusing to pay your council tax until they reinstate the old-style wheelie bins.'

Patrick let out a rasping chuckle. 'And every time I take out the rubbish I still think those bins are just too damn small!'

Phil noted his father's rucksack. 'Do you want a few minutes to nip up to your room and drop that off, Dad? You don't want to be carrying it around all day.'

'I'm fine thanks, son,' replied his dad, squeezing the strap of his bag. 'It's got my angina medicine in it, so I'll keep it with me to be on the safe side.'

Following Simon's lead Phil, Patrick and the boys made their way outside the hotel. It was another bright, sunny day – classic T-shirt weather – and although Phil still felt like death warmed up his spirits couldn't fail to be lifted by the vividness of the cloudless blue sky above their heads as he slipped on his sunglasses.

The good weather had drawn the inhabitants of Amsterdam into the city centre as well as those there for the weekend. There was a buzz about the city as people got on and off tram cars, stood in crowds watching English-speaking outdoor theatre performers or simply sat watching the world go by outside numerous cafés and restaurants.

The boys having dismissed several possible breakfast venues on the basis that they 'didn't look right', finally came to a halt outside a pub off Dam Square. It was called the Shamrock Inn and had two faded Guinness posters blu-tacked to the glass doors at the entrance. Phil tried to keep his mouth shut but he just couldn't help himself. 'You come all the way to Amsterdam and this is the place you want to eat your first meal of the day?'

'It does English breakfasts,' said Degsy. 'We can't come on a stag weekend and not have a full English breakfast. It'd be criminal.'

'The lad's right,' said Patrick. 'I've had breakfasts all round the world from Bangkok to Wilmington Ohio and I haven't had one better than the Great British breakfast. It's one of the few things we do well.'

Reuben, Spencer and Deano nodded in agreement.

Phil hoped that at least Simon might be the voice of reason. 'Come on Si,' he encouraged, 'You know this is wrong.'

Simon shrugged. 'Mate,' he said wearily, 'I'm starving

and my head feels like it got hit by a truck. I don't care what we eat or where we eat it as long as we eat it now.'

The debate concluded, they took a table between a scruffy-looking British couple sipping tea from large mugs that said 'I love London', and five lads in their late teens tucking into a plate of sausage sandwiches while broadcasting in braying public school accents the highlights of the sex show they had been to the night before.

Clearly working on the basis that targeting people with hangovers would keep the people who cared about the provenance of their sausages far away, the Shamrock Inn's English breakfast was as disappointing as it was overpriced. The eggs were pale and undercooked, the bacon hopelessly chewy, the toast cold, the bright orange baked beans congealed and the sausages little more than cereal rusk and mechanically recovered meat stuffed into a flimsy casing.

Phil ate no more than three mouthfuls of his breakfast before abandoning it in favour of a mug of tepid sugary tea, which he drained in three gulps.

'Not hungry?' asked Spencer spying Phil's full plate.

'Nah,' said Phil. 'I think I've lost my appetite.'

'So can I . . . ?' Spencer nodded towards the food. 'Shame to see it go to waste.'

'Help yourself, mate.'

Not needing to be told twice, Spencer shared out the leftovers among the grateful boys.

Phil stood up and stretched. The thought of spending

the next ten minutes watching the others eat breakfast was about as appealing as eating the breakfast himself. 'I'm going to go for a walk,' he said. 'Clear my head a bit. Are you guys going to be here for a while or shall we just meet up later?'

'Hang on a sec and I'll come with you,' said Simon as the boys murmured that they wouldn't be going anywhere soon. 'I'm not ready to start drinking but I could do with getting hold of some fags.'

Donning their sunglasses the two friends headed towards Dam Square in silence, content, it seemed, to allow the sights and sounds around them to be their entertainment.

'You're hating this, aren't you?' said Simon as they passed a group of kids splashing each other in one of the square's fountains. 'I can see it on your face.'

'I'm not hating it, exactly,' replied Phil.

'But you're not loving it either?'

Phil shook his head. 'No,' he said, 'not if I'm honest.'

'So what can I do to make it right?' They passed an elderly couple throwing bread to a flock of increasingly aggressive pigeons. 'I don't want to ruin things for you, mate. It's supposed to be your weekend after all.'

'Well the boys seem to be having a laugh. I'm just being a bit of a misery that's all.'

'And I'm guessing from the way you were knocking back the hard stuff last night that you were a bit freaked out by that girl turning out to be Aiden Reid's ex-missus.'

'Just a bit. It's not her so much as him. I've never

even met the guy, but sometimes it seems like he's everywhere I go.'

'You've said in the past that you thought Helen might still—'

'That was ages ago,' said Phil cutting him off. 'And I don't think that any more. Me and Helen couldn't be any more rock solid if we tried.'

'So what's the problem then?'

'There isn't one.'

Simon laughed. 'You'll have to do better than that. Remember I've known you a long time.'

They passed a middle-aged man wearing a Manchester United top fast asleep against one of the lion statues. 'Fine,' said Phil as the man stirred. 'The thing is I'm thinking about seeing Sanne. The girl from last night.'

'Why would you do that? Because you want to know about him? Then read a paper, mate. He's in there every other day.'

Phil came to a halt next to a bench but didn't sit down. 'I knew you wouldn't get it.'

'Of course I don't get it,' said Simon, 'there's nothing to get. Why would you want to go winding yourself up over your missus's ex a week before you're getting married? Makes no sense.'

'And leaving your wife and kids does?'

'You don't know all the facts.'

'Then why don't you tell me them?' said Phil, with more than a hint of anger in his voice. 'I'm your mate, aren't I? You're my best man. What proof do you need that I'm on your side?'

'It's not that easy.'

'That doesn't mean you can't try.'

'I can't, mate.'

'Can't or won't?'

'Does it matter?'

'To me it does, yeah. I know you think this isn't any of my business and maybe you're right, but if the tables were turned you'd be having a go at me. I know you would.'

Simon bit his lip in frustration and then in a sudden burst of resignation, said: 'You want the truth? Well here it is: I've fallen in love with someone else.'

'Fallen in love? Who with?'

Simon shook his head. 'Believe me when I say mate, that you do not want to know.'

'Well maybe I do.'

'No,' said Simon firmly, 'you don't.'

'At this point we should agree to disagree but that's just not going to happen is it,' said Phil. 'I'm not going to let this go, Si, I'm not. So just tell me, okay? It's not Reuben's missus is it?'

'No, no of course not.'

'Then who?'

'I can't.'

'Yes, you can. All you've got to do is say the name and it's done.'

A group of teenage girls passed by singing in Dutch at the top of their voices.

'It's Caitlin,' said Simon. He looked Phil in the eyes. 'I'm sorry mate,' he continued, 'I'm really sorry. I didn't mean for it to happen, it was just one of those things.'

'One of what things?' exploded Phil. 'You haven't actually told me anything yet!'

'Look, mate,' said Simon backing away, 'we don't need to talk about this. You know now and that's all that matters.'

Phil stepped towards Simon. 'You think you can get away with leaving it like that?

'I don't want to talk about it now, that's all,' said Simon. 'This is *your* weekend.'

'And Caitlin's *my* sister,' said Phil, advancing so far into Simon's personal space that he could smell the tea on his friend's breath. 'How long has this been going on? Months? Weeks?' Simon shrugged and took a step back. Phil repeated his question: 'How long?'

Simon cast his eyes down to the cobblestones. 'Since before Easter.'

Phil cast his mind back to the time in question. 'Deano's birthday?' Simon nodded. 'You were talking to her loads that night I remember.' Phil shook his head in disbelief. 'That's my kid sister!'

'I know,' said Simon. 'I feel awful about it. I really do.'

'But not awful enough to keep your hands off her!'

'It wasn't like that.'

'No,' said Phil. 'It never is, is it? When were you going to tell me? When you moved in with her? Was I supposed to drop in to see her, see your shoes in the hallway and put two and two together?'

'You know it wasn't like that,' stammered Simon, 'I just couldn't find the right time to tell you.'

Phil's face was the picture of disbelief. 'And you've been carrying on like this ever since Deano's do?'

'Sort of.'

'Sort of? What does that mean? Whatever it is you have to say, just spit it out.'

'It's complicated.'

'Complicated how?'

'She ended it about a month ago.'

Phil breathed a sigh of relief. 'So it's over?'

'Not for me.'

'And what's that supposed to mean?'

'It means,' said Simon solemnly, 'that I love her. I really love her.'

'And that's why you've left Yaz and the kids, is it?' scoffed Phil. 'Because you think you're in love with Caitlin? You do know what sort of girl Caitlin is, don't you? You do know that there are half a dozen blokes around the country who all think that they can't live without her. Come on Si, I love her to bits but even I know that she's a total bitch when it comes to men. She uses them. She always has done and probably always will. She likes their money and their attention but the second she's bored she's off and – be under no illusions about this – she won't come back.'

'You don't know that,' said Simon. 'Her and me together, it was special. Really special.'

'So what? You're leaving Yaz and your kids to prove your commitment to Cait in the hope that she'll take you back?' Phil felt genuine pity for his friend but also like he might throw a punch at any moment. 'I need to get out of here.'

Simon shrugged. 'What do you want me to tell the others?'

'Tell 'em what you told me,' snapped Phil, 'and see where that gets you.'

9.

Back at the hotel, Phil headed straight up to his room. The door was open and the chambermaid's cart was parked directly outside. He shuddered at the thought of her reaction to the chaos within, and again at what she would have seen had he not had the foresight to hide the stolen penumatic drill.

Apologising for disturbing her, Phil began searching for the piece of paper with Sanne's number on, that he'd screwed up and left on the table next to the TV. It wasn't there. The chambermaid must have dumped it. He spotted a large bin bag on the floor and began frantically rooting through it. Used tissues. Plastic bags. Sandwich wrappers. Half-empty water bottles. The rotting remains of a fruit salad. On the point of giving up Phil delved one last time and there, still screwed up in a ball was Sanne's number.

Phil held it open with one hand while he reached for the phone with the other and then tried to work out what exactly to say to Sanne. The essence of which was that having endured the triple whammy of a raging hangover, having his sixty-six-year-old dad join his stag weekend and discovering that his married best man had been sleeping with his sister, he now wanted to spend time in the company of someone who couldn't surprise him with any more revelations. And while he appreciated that Sanne by virtue of her association with Aiden Reid had already knocked him sideways with a revelation of her own, the fact remained that he needed to get away from both friends and family, and as Sanne was neither, she was his safest bet.

'Hello?'

The line wasn't great and neither was his recall of her voice hidden as it had been for most of the night under the constant thump of the blandest of club music.

'Hi, Sanne, it's me,' said Phil. 'The English guy from last night.'

Sanne laughed. 'You say that like you imagine I gave out my number to so many people last night that I might have forgotten! How are you? I hope you didn't run into those guys again. Did you have a good night?'

Phil's head throbbed at the very thought of it. 'It was fine, thanks. And no, we didn't see those guys again. How about yours?'

'It was good fun. It's always nice to catch up with friends that you haven't seen in a long while. So, I take it you're calling because you want to take up my offer?'

'Definitely, if it's still there.'

There was a short pause and then she said: 'I can probably spare you an hour if you'd like. I thought I was going to have longer but a friend called this morning with a boyfriend crisis. You know how it is, she needs me to do the whole shoulder to cry on thing.'

'An hour's fine,' said Phil. 'Do you still think the Van Gogh Museum is the place to go?'

'Absolutely. It'll take me a little while to get ready and cycle over there so how does an hour from now sound?'

'Perfect.'

'Meet me at the entrance. Do you need directions?'

'No,' said Phil making a mental note to get hold of a guidebook. 'I'm sure I'll be fine.'

It was a little after one in the afternoon as Phil, having got lost several times along the way, finally reached his destination. Pulling his jacket and shirt, damp with perspiration, away from his back, Phil scanned the crowds milling outside the entrance to the museum but couldn't see Sanne anywhere. Deciding to find a shop and buy a bottle of water he was about to cross the road when he felt a tap on the shoulder, and turned around to see Sanne.

She was wheeling a bike which, unlike the thousands he had seen so far this weekend was a bright metallic pink, rather than black, and had a basket on the front decorated with plastic roses.

She was once again looking head-turningly attractive, wearing sunglasses, a light blue floral dress and gold sandals and he wondered how he could not have realised that she was famous when standing next to her now it was impossible to imagine that she could be anything but.

'So, you found your way here without too much trouble?' she asked, taking in his suit without comment.

'I have a killer sense of direction,' joked Phil. 'I should have been a boy scout.'

'But you weren't?'

'What?'

'A boy scout?'

Phil shook his head. Why had he even mentioned boy scouts in the first place? 'I was a sea cadet for a while when I was fourteen,' he explained, 'but after six weeks without seeing so much as the inside of a canoe I reasoned that it wasn't for me.'

'I was what we call in the Netherlands a *Padvindster*,' she explained as they walked towards the museum entrance. 'It's like your Girl Guides in the UK. At the end of each meeting we'd have to say: ' "I am a link in the golden chain of world friendship, and I will keep my link strong and bright." '

'And did you?'

Sanne laughed. 'I most certainly did!'

The queue for the museum seemed to be moving quite briskly. At a loss for what to talk about, Phil opted to fall back on the weather.

'The weather this weekend has been amazing hasn't it?'

Sanne smiled and looked at her watch. 'I bet myself that you'd mention the weather within five minutes of us meeting and I was right!'

Only a little embarrassed by his poor conversational

skills Phil attempted to make a defence. 'Well, it is a nice day!'

'The Dutch aren't like this,' continued Sanne. 'We notice the weather but never feel the need to go on and on about it like the English. That's one of the things I actually miss about not living in the UK any more. In England there's always a way of making conversation with anyone no matter who they are or what they do.'

'Well, since we're on the subject of national stereotypes,' grinned Phil, 'when exactly did they make it obligatory for Dutch people to ride bikes? Do you get given one at birth?'

'So, you'd rather we went everywhere by car like you do in the UK?' countered Sanne. 'I'd never seen people drive such short distances until I lived in your country. Need a pack of fags . . . jump in the car. Need a stamp . . . jump in a car. One day the English will grow wheels.'

'It's because in the old days an Englishman's home was his castle,' explained Phil. 'These days his castle is more likely to be his Ford Mondeo. So,' he said leaping on the first subject that came to mind, 'is Van Gogh a particular favourite of yours?'

Sanne nodded. 'Everybody in Holland loves Van Gogh,' she replied. 'He is our country's favourite son. Why? Do you not like him?'

Phil shrugged. 'I don't know much about him beyond him lopping off his ear, having Don McLean write a song about him and that Kirk Douglas once played him in a film.'

Sanne was scandalised. 'You don't study art in UK schools?'

Phil recalled the level of artistic debate that had existed at his local comprehensive. 'Not the one I went to.'

'Was yours a special school of some kind?'

'That would be one word for it,' joked Phil. 'Put it this way, it was a bit rough. Not the kind of school where there was a lot of talk about art.'

'And since then?'

'What?'

'You've done no learning about art?'

'Not really,' he replied. 'I've been to the art gallery in Nottingham a few times and watched the odd documentary on TV but I wouldn't really say I've learned about it. I'd like to though. I've always felt like – much like with music and film – the world would be a poorer place without it.'

'Do you have any pictures on your walls at home?'

'A few, but they're mainly things that my girlfriend bought.'

'So she's the artistic one in your relationship?'

'Yeah,' said Phil, wondering what Helen would say if she could see him standing in the queue outside the Van Gogh Museum with a beautiful, famous Dutch girl who just happened to be Aiden Reid's ex-wife. 'I suppose you could say she is.'

They reached the ticket desk and Phil paid for two tickets. They went inside, checked in their bags and passed through the security scanners into the first gallery, which Sanne explained was dedicated to paintings by artists who were friends, contemporaries or were considered an inspiration to the young Van Gogh.

As they worked their way around the room studying each painting Phil read a few of the names on the wall beside the paintings. Being here with an actual art lover made him feel more keenly what he always felt whenever he went to museums or art galleries: that he was on the outside looking in at people who spoke a language no one had taken the time to teach him.

Sanne, he observed, understood the language of art perfectly. Every now and again she would stand in front of a picture over which Phil had passed a cursory glance and would tilt her head slightly to one side and bite her lip absentmindedly as though she was lost deep inside the painting. He had seen Helen do the same thing and although he had tried with her help to make that connection with a work of art, most of the time he had felt nothing.

As they wandered through the galleries on the upper floors which divided Van Gogh's work chronologically, somewhere around 1880 Phil's mind began to drift. Chief amongst the thoughts that sought to occupy him was what his friends were up to and what excuse Simon dreamed up for his absence. Knowing Simon, the excuse would be sufficiently vague not to cause alarm and with his father present to act as the entertainment, they would hardly miss him. Phil had no idea what that afternoon's activity might be but even though he didn't seem to be getting very much from seeing the work of one of the world's greatest artists first-hand it had to be better than getting stoned or gawping at the girls in the windows of the brothels in De Wallen.

'You don't seem to be enjoying yourself,' said Sanne as they entered the final gallery, Auvers – 1890. 'You look a bit bored.'

'Not bored,' replied Phil. 'Just disappointed I suppose. In myself, not him. Given that this is the year he tops himself and I've yet to be moved by any of the paintings I've got a horrible feeling that art isn't for me at all.'

'I used to have a friend just like you,' said Sanne. 'He was a really dynamic guy, and he loved all sorts of culture but he never got art. And when I brought him here he said exactly the same thing right until the very end.'

'And then what happened?'

'I showed him my favourite picture.'

Phil's curiosity knew no bounds, convinced as he was that the 'friend' was Aiden Reid.

The painting depicted a bright yellow wheat field with three paths in it underneath a dark foreboding sky. Phil stared at it long and hard imagining himself standing next to the painter, seeing what he was seeing and feeling what he was feeling.

'What do you think?' asked Sanne.

Phil thought hard. He felt lots of things but nothing he cared to put into words. 'I think your friend was right,' he said quietly as he imagined Aiden Reid standing in front of this very picture. 'One single picture really can change your mind about everything.'

'I really want to thank you for that,' said Phil as they stood in the shade of the museum. Most of the hour she had promised him had gone by now. 'I never expected to enjoy looking around here as much as I did.'

'My pleasure,' said Sanne. 'Always glad to add another convert to the Van Gogh army.'

'Well, should you find yourself in Nottingham I'll gladly return the favour,' replied Phil, 'although the best we can do is a statue of Robin Hood who might not even have existed.'

Sanne laughed. 'Or we could get a drink if you've got time.'

'But I thought you needed to—' Sanne looked guilty and the penny dropped. 'There was no friend in urgent need of a shoulder, was there?'

'Oh, come on,' protested Sanne, 'don't look at me like that! I met you in a queue outside a bar! I didn't know anything about you!'

They walked across a wide, open area which Sanne informed him was known as Museumplein towards a large paddling pool crammed full of parents and young children splashing in the water. To the right of the pool was their destination, a café with a large terrace: and ducking inside out of the glare of the sun they re-emerged, carrying an iced coffee and a Coke and sat down at a table in the shade of a huge awning.

Phil tried to coax out more of Sanne's personal

history even though he was already aware of the salient parts of it. She was, he learned, currently working part-time as a dance teacher specialising in modern, tap and ballet but prior to that had worked in the music business over in the UK. These days as far as the singing went she gigged at clubs in and around Amsterdam doing what she described as 'a kind of acoustic, twenty-first century Joni Mitchell thing'. Curious to see how reluctant she might be to tell him about her previous fame Phil attempted to get her to be more specific but all she would say was that the work had involved 'music videos, backing vocals and the like', and that although it had been fun at the time she had no regrets that this period of her life was over.

'So what brought you back to Amsterdam?' he asked. 'Or is that too personal a question?'

'No, it's fine,' she replied. 'My marriage ended and I felt the only place I might be able to heal would be back home.'

'I'm sorry to hear that,' replied Phil, meaning it. 'He must be an idiot, your ex-husband.'

Sanne smiled. 'That's kind of you to say so,' she said. 'But it was a bit more complicated than that.'

Phil just couldn't help himself. 'How so?'

'You can't really be interested.'

'You'd be surprised,' replied Phil. 'Despite what you saw last night, I'm a lover not a fighter. So come on then, what was the reason?'

'All the time he was with me he was in love with someone else . . . someone from his past.'

'An ex?'

She nodded. 'Yes, an ex.'

Phil's chest tightened. 'I know this is going to sound weird,' he began, 'but does this woman have a name? I'm just curious I suppose, I'm just trying to picture the kind of woman that would have that sort of effect on a guy.'

'Helen,' said Sanne quietly, 'her name was Helen.'

10.

Phil was standing in front of the sink in the café's gents' toilets frantically splashing water on his face, like people do in films when trying to regain their composure after a shock. If this had been a film, maybe the water-splashing would have done the trick and allowed him to return to the table outside and act like a normal human being but as it wasn't a film, but real life in all its Technicolor glory, he just managed to drench the front of his shirt and part of his tie, earning himself a number of odd looks.

Aiden Reid's marriage had collapsed because of Helen. That had been the long and the short of what Sanne had said, hadn't it? After all those years, after all that time, Helen's ex's feelings for her had remained so strong that they had overcome what he felt for Sanne, his wife. Did Helen know that Aiden felt this way? Had he tried to contact her after his marriage ended or even while they were still together? Phil tried to recall when he had read in the papers about Sanne and Aiden Reid separating. Last year? The year before? He recalled past occasions when Helen had seemed out of sorts. Like the period when for weeks on end she would get up in the middle of the night and watch TV claiming that the stress of working under a new station manager was affecting her sleep patterns or the time before that when he would find her in tears in the darkness of their bedroom. She'd claimed it was because she was worried about her dad's struggle with Alzheimer's or her mother's upcoming operation. There were more such incidents and although each came with a perfectly plausible explanation Phil wondered if at least one of them had been due to Aiden Reid.

Phil suddenly felt tired and hungover again. He was too old to be plagued by this kind of insecurity. He didn't need thoughts of some oily celebrity stalking his girlfriend a week before his own wedding. Whether Aiden had contacted Helen or not, he knew Helen would never let him down. He did know that, didn't he? In all the years they had been together, making a home together, she had never given him any cause to doubt her loyalty. Helen had chosen him as the man that she wanted to be with for all time. They were getting married. This time next week he would be putting a ring on her finger.

Feeling more positive after his internal pep talk Phil wiped his face on a paper towel, made his way outside and stood for a moment observing Sanne watching two small children taking turns to chase each other around the children's playground a few feet from their table. It was a shame. Her beauty, former fame and connection to Aiden Reid aside, she was actually really easy to get on with and perhaps in a different life they could have been friends.

'I'd better be getting off,' said Phil as he reached the table.

'Oh,' said Sanne rising to her feet, 'are you sure? I was just thinking that if you really wanted to see Amsterdam I could show you around Vondelpark. It's not far at all.'

'That's really kind of you,' replied Phil, 'but I've got to go. The boys . . . well you know, I'm supposed to be on a stag weekend . . .'

Sanne smiled. 'Yes, of course. You should go.' She kissed his cheek. 'It was lovely to meet you Philip Hudson, it really was and I wish you and your wife all the happiness in the world.' She handed Phil a club flyer from her bag. 'A parting gift from me to you! It's a gig I'm doing tonight at the Yellow Robot, it's an acoustic thing. I'm pretty sure it won't be to your friends' liking but if you do get a chance to drop in you should say hi.'

He felt relieved and guilty as he walked away. Pleasant though she was, she was the gateway to a very special kind of madness that he could do without. For the rest of the weekend at least he would forget all about art, culture and the pursuit of deeper meaning for his time in Amsterdam and join his friends in the things that really mattered on a stag weekend: having a laugh and getting trashed.

Keen to get out of the sun for a while, Phil caught a tram to get him closer to the hotel, alighting at

Amsterdam Centraal. The city centre was crawling with a heady mixture of locals and tourists. Outside the station Phil spotted a crowd being entertained by a mime artist duo whose skin, clothes and hair were covered in silver paint and he felt a sudden pang for Helen. If she had been with him they would have stopped to enjoy the spectacle before heading off somewhere nice for a canalside drink.

Right now Phil needed to hear Helen's voice more than anything in the world. He missed her and wanted, if only for the duration of a three-minute call to be connected to her in some meaningful way. He scanned the square for a public phone and eventually found one back in the station next to a bank of ticket machines.

Phil pulled out some loose change and dropped the coins in the slot. He was about to tap the first digit of Helen's number into the keypad when the fatal flaw in his plan dawned on him. Although he could remember all manner of phone numbers from his Nan's before she moved into a home, to the office fax which hadn't been used in a decade, the one number he couldn't recall was Helen's.

It wasn't just that he only ever called Helen's mobile from his own, it was also that Helen had lost her phone or changed providers so many times that he couldn't even begin to guess what it might be. Was there a double seven in there somewhere? He felt sure there was, and of course it would start with a zero, but other than that, he just kept drawing a blank.

Returning the receiver to its cradle, Phil scooped the

coins out of the tray and headed back outside into the sunshine. One of the silver-painted mime artists, waved at him robotically, and Phil dug into his trouser pockets for the very same coins he had hoped to use talking to his fiancée, and dropped them into the silver hat at their feet.

Phil stepped through the revolving doors of the hotel into the air-conditioned cool of the lobby. He was boiling in his suit, and his head still ached and all he wanted was to go to bed for a couple of hours but as he came around the corner he walked straight into the boys and his father coming in the opposite direction.

'Big man!' bellowed Deano. 'Where you been?'

'I . . . er . . . I,' Phil's voice trailed off as he noticed that the boys were no longer in their suits but dressed in tracksuits and trainers. 'What's with the gear? Are we playing footie or something?'

'Better than footie mate!' chipped in Spencer. 'Paintball.'

'Paintball?'

Phil looked at Simon. He was lurking at the back next to Patrick and Reuben looking down at the floor but clearly paying attention to what was being said. 'Is that really what we're doing, Si?'

Obviously still smarting from their earlier encounter Simon nodded once but didn't utter a syllable.

'Mate,' said Spencer excitedly. 'We looked up the place at an internet café after we finished breakfast and it looks ace!'

'He's not wrong either!' added Reuben. 'This place is

the business. Loads of different scenarios, a big full-on battle at the end and one hundred paintballs included in the price. It's like everything you ever wanted back when you were a kid.'

Spencer did a little dance. 'It's true, fella,' he said cheerfully. 'I can't wait! It'll be like *Black Hawk Down* mashed with *Saving Private Ryan*. But don't worry bro' I've got your back! No man left behind!'

Phil thought hard even though Spencer hadn't actually asked a question. Did he really want to spend a sweltering afternoon in a tracksuit running around some abandoned farm in some unknown location in Amsterdam with the mother of all hangovers? Phil had been paintballing many times and had always hated it on the grounds that, for reasons he could never quite fathom, he somehow managed to get shot in the first five minutes of the game. The thought of adding an unspecified number of assailants (many of whom would be suffering from raging hangovers), to what was already a pretty dangerous game, made him feel ill.

He looked at his dad. 'You're not doing it too, are you?'

His father let out an emphysemic chuckle. 'I'd like to see the man who would be able to stop me!'

'Fine,' said Phil, 'give me five and I'll be right with you.'

The BattleZone Paintball Centre was everything Phil feared and more. Located on the outskirts of Amsterdam on several acres of wood and farmland, it was staffed by needlessly muscular English-speaking Dutch guys dressed like extras from a Chuck Norris film. There were life-sized posters of soldiers from every major Special Forces unit in the world on the walls in the main reception and painted on its front door were the words: 'No guts, no glory.' It was a solitary beacon in what passed for the Dutch countryside to British stag parties city wide to come, shoot and be merry, and could only have been more successful with this demographic had it actually been situated in Leidseplein or in De Wallen.

Once they had registered Phil, the boys and his dad were ushered into a large, empty hangar with about fifteen stag parties, all of them British. The instructors explained the dos and don'ts of paintball but Phil was distracted by the fact that a number of his fellow combatants were paying the instructors no attention at all, grinning inanely at the cache of weapons about to be distributed. This, thought Phil, did not bode well for the afternoon ahead.

Because of the numbers involved (and presumably to cut down on the risk of anyone actually being killed) all the individual stag parties were divided in two, to form two new teams, Delta Black and Cobra Red, and given their first mission 'Operation Relic' in which they had to rescue an ancient statue from a recently crashed plane on an abandoned airfield. It was, Phil noted wearily, essentially a 'grab the flag and get it back to your own base without getting killed' type scenario that he had played dozens of times before.

With orders in place all the men were handed overalls, kneepads, facemasks, coloured armbands and fully loaded paintball guns. They were instructed to meet at their respective command centres at opposite ends of the playing field (which for the purposes of authenticity had been made to look like an abandoned airfield).

Phil watched as members of Delta Black including Simon, Deano and Spencer exited the hangar with the rest of their team leaving Phil with his dad, Reuben, Degsy and a bunch of blokes he had never met before to make their way to their own base camp.

On the way a man in his mid-twenties with a crew cut and a partially visible neck tattoo struck up conversation with Phil.

'You done this before, mate?' he asked with a Bristol accent so strong Phil thought for a moment that he might be putting it on.

'Nah, mate,' said Phil. It occurred to him that he ought to return the question if only out of politeness. 'You?'

'Me and my mates back home do it every weekend.'

'Really?' replied Phil, relieved at not having to face this tattooed weekend warrior on the battlefield. 'So, how would you advise me to stay alive as long as possible then?'

The young man grinned, lowered the mask that had been sitting on his head and with a muffled voice said: 'Kick arse, mate, it always seems to work for me!'

With the profundity of his comrade's advice still echoing around his head Phil reached base camp where a Scouser called Jason appeared to have elected himself commanding officer.

'You lot over there take the right side,' he said pointing at one group, 'you lot over there take the left side,' he said pointing to another, 'and me and these guys,' he said gesturing to Phil's party and the few who remained, 'will cover you both and advance at the same time.'

It seemed no one had either the will or the desire to argue with Jason, so once the whistle was blown for the commencement of the battle his orders were followed to the letter.

For a while Phil couldn't tell what was happening. He could hear a lot of shouting and the sound of paintball pellets whistling overhead but as for how many people had been shot and who was closest to getting to the statue from the aeroplane he had no idea.

Phil would have been content to remain hidden in their sandbag dugout firing the odd paintball bullet in the air for the rest of the game but after about five minutes Jason nudged Phil sharply in the ribs and whispered hoarsely, 'Let's go for it!' and before he knew what was happening he was being dragged over the top through the middle of the battlefield in the direction of the plane.

It seemed as though every last member of Delta Black was firing in their direction and Phil was convinced that it was only a miracle that neither of them had been hit before they reached a sandbag dug-out a few metres from the tail of the plane. Relieved, they stopped to take a breather but then the shots stopped and through a gap in the sandbags Phil made out a figure that was unmistakably Simon making a break for the door of the plane.

For reasons that Phil didn't want to analyse the thought that Simon might be about to win the game for his team filled him with rage. Who was this guy who felt that everything was his for the taking? Who was this guy who thought that it was okay to take up with his best mate's sister when there was a world full of unrelated women? Whoever this guy was he needed taking down, and he needed taking down now. Without a second thought Phil leapt over the sandbags screaming, 'Not on my watch!!!' at the top of his voice and ran full pelt across the open space to the plane without getting hit.

Spying Simon about to make a grab for the statue Phil released an extensive volley of paintballs in his friend's direction so that in mere moments his face and body were splattered with bright luminous yellow paint.

'I'm dead!' screamed Simon thrusting his hands in the air in defeat. 'You've got me! I'm dead!'

'I don't care!' screamed Phil, as he continued to unload paintball after paintball into Simon's head far closer than the regulation five-metre minimum distance they had been advised, 'I just want you to grow a pair, go back to your wife and stop poking my sodding sister!'

11.

The conversation in the minibus on the way back into central Amsterdam was muted to say the least. Simon sat up front with the driver glowering at any passerby who had the misfortune to catch his eye, while Phil was at the back doing pretty much the same. Between them sat the boys and Phil's dad, who while not being fully conversant with everything that had brought 'Operation Relic' to its abrupt conclusion were aware that *something* had gone on and that there was a very good chance that the 'something' in question was connected with Phil's earlier disappearance.

Phil was busy examining his own behaviour. The news that Simon had left Yaz for Caitlin had obviously upset him more than he had initially thought and the unacknowledged aggression that he felt towards his friend had manifested itself during the paintball game. As a result, his best man had not only suffered severe bruising around the chest area but also the beginnings of a black eye.

But was that all there was to it? Yes, Simon had felt the force of Phil's anger, but had he been the only source? Wasn't at least some of the anger directed at Aiden Reid, who, despite Phil's attempt to keep him under lock and key, had somehow managed to escape and was now wreaking havoc in the darker reaches of his mind? Phil just wanted to live in a world free of stress. A place where his best mate hadn't left his wife in order to sleep with his sister and his fiancée's ex wasn't so in love with her that he had allowed his marriage to fall apart because of it. None of this would have come to light if they had stuck to his original plan and gone go-karting followed by a pint and curry in Beeston.

The tension between Phil and Simon showed no sign of waning as the boys alighted from the minibus. Because it was clear that Simon (who usually acted as leader/tour organiser) wouldn't be doing a great deal of leading/tour organising any time soon Deano stepped into the power vacuum that had been created and as they all hovered in the lobby, set out his plan for the evening.

'Here's what we're going to do,' he announced. 'We're going to take an hour to clean up, wash, get a bit of kip and get ready, then it's back down here at seven on the dot to grab a tram to Leidseplein. Agreed?'

Although the closest Deano got to a verbal agreement was a grunt from Simon it was implicit from the absence of any alternative that his plan had been passed unanimously and so one by one the boys dispersed leaving Phil standing alone.

Keen to avoid further confrontation with his best man, Phil took the stairs to his room and quickly stepped inside. Leaning against the door he gradually allowed his feet to slip from underneath him until he'd completely collapsed on the carpet.

Phil had no idea how long he sat scrunched up at the base of the door but it was certainly long enough for his legs to become so numb that he had to crawl to the bathroom for his second shower of the day.

He threw on some underwear and lay down on the bed, going over events in increasing amounts of detail. He felt his eyelids become heavier and his breathing shallower until he was just a few breaths away from unconsciousness when, completely unbidden, a partial mobile phone number popped up in his mind's eye and even though parts of it were indistinct he knew it was Helen's.

Bolt upright now Phil grabbed the phone by the side of the bed and tapped in the few numbers he could recall before they faded from memory. The first six numbers came as easily as if he had been reading them but the next three felt glued to the inside of his skull and needed to be forcibly ripped out with his fingertips. The last two remained complete mysteries. He stared at the keypad hoping the digits might leap out at him. He eventually pressed a four and then a two and waited.

'Hello?'

A man's voice, a Midlands accent, yet even so he didn't want to give up hope.

'Is Helen there?'

'Don't know any Helen mate,' said the man. 'You must have the wrong number.'

The line went dead. With a heavy heart Phil put down the receiver and manoeuvred himself under the bed covers. It had been a long day, and a lot had happened, maybe everything would look better after a good sleep. As he closed his eyes and waited for sleep there was a sharp knock at the door.

Phil ignored the knock and put a pillow over his head but then a second knock came, this time even louder. Rubbing his eyes and feeling heavy of limb Phil crawled out of bed, grabbed the door handle and twisted it open. The door was barely more than a fraction ajar when there was a loud grunt from the other side and the door burst open, sending Phil flying to the floor.

Bewildered, Phil saw Simon's huge form descending on him as if they were in the opening bout of a WWE wrestling tournament. There was no time to move out of the way so he braced himself for the impact and hoped that his friend wouldn't do too much damage.

Phil didn't waste valuable energy trying to work out why his best man had kicked opened his door and was trying to pummel him into submission. Simon was wrestling with him for one reason and one reason only: he had grown tired of the energy required to sulk and had made up his mind that they should sort out the situation man to man.

It was, to be truthful, far from the most gainly of altercations by anybody's standards and had more in common with a documentary Phil had once seen on the mating rituals of otters than it did with Hollywood style punch-ups with their over the top sound effects and dynamic kung-fu poses. This was simply two men, in their late thirties, who knew that they had work on Monday, pretending to fight when all they were really doing was minimising each other's attempts to deliver a blow that might actually cause lasting damage.

It didn't take long for them to realise that now Simon had lost the element of surprise, they were so equally matched that it was pointless for them to continue wrestling. Both were regulars at the gym and while Simon was taller, Phil was more muscular so, much like two equally matched tug o' war teams, they cancelled each other out.

'Truce?' called Simon from inside Phil's headlock.

'Thought you'd never ask,' replied Phil as Simon released his crushing grip from around Phil's waist.

The two men lay on their backs panting as if they had both run a marathon. Simon grinned at his friend. 'That was pathetic wasn't it?'

'Too embarrassing for words,' said Phil rubbing his rib cage. 'We should keep this just between the two of us.'

'I've already locked it in the vault,' said Simon. He held out his hand. 'Mates?'

Phil knocked Simon's hand away and stood up. 'Don't think for a second that this makes things right between us. You've been banging my sister you tosspot. I'll never forgive you for that.'

'And you shot me in the head with a paintball at point blank range!' defended Simon. 'Have you seen my face? I look like I've gone twelve rounds with Mike Tyson!'

Phil looked at the bruising on Simon's face and smiled. 'I did get you good and proper, didn't I?'

'You think that's bad you should see my back. It's like I've been trampled by a rhino.'

Phil sat down on the bed. He wasn't sure he had the energy to stay annoyed with Simon for the whole weekend. 'If it's any consolation,' he conceded, 'I'd say a good seventy-five per cent of the aggression I unleashed at you was actually meant for someone else.'

Simon closed the bedroom door and sat down on the bed. 'Who? Your dad? What's he done now?'

Phil shook his head. 'Not dad, though that's not to say he couldn't do with shooting. I'm talking about Aiden Reid.'

'What about him? He's a twat, let it go, move on.'

'I would do,' began Phil, 'but . . . well . . . after I left you and the guys this morning I met up with that Sanne girl from last night.'

'And did what?'

'Walked around the Van Gogh Museum for the most part. Did you know he shot himself in the chest because he was depressed but it still took two days for him to die?'

'Do you fancy her?'

'Who?'

'Who do you think? She's bloody gorgeous!'

'Honest mate,' replied Phil. 'It's not like that.'

'So enlighten me.'

'I needed to get away – from you mainly – and so like

I said we went to the museum and then afterwards to a café and talked.'

'And what did she say that got you riled up enough to want to shoot me in the head?'

'She told me the reason that she and Aiden Reid split up,' said Phil looking down at the floor, 'was because he was still in love with someone from his past. I asked her this woman's name and she told me there on the spot: Helen.'

'So what did she say when you told her who you were? She must have been well freaked out.'

'I didn't. Like you said it would be too weird. I mean what are the chances of me chatting to some random woman in a queue outside a bar only to discover that she's my fiancée's ex's ex-wife.'

'But that's what actually happened!'

'I know,' replied Phil, 'but she'd never believe it would she? Anyway, she's playing a gig tonight and I'm thinking about seeing her again. I need to know the full story. I need to know if he's been in contact with Helen or even if he's capable of doing something reckless like turning up at the wedding next week. He's a proper full-on celebrity, Si, he drives Ferraris and interviews Hollywood stars and hangs out with footballers and to top it all he's Helen's first love. How am I going to compete with all that unless I arm myself with as much info as I can?'

There was a silence and then Simon stood up. 'Mate . . . I'm going to tell you something and I want you to listen hard, okay?'

Phil nodded. 'Okay.'

Simon put a hand on each of Phil's shoulders and stared into his eyes. 'Stop being an idiot.'

'But—'

Simon held his hand up in the air. 'No ifs, no buts, just stop it and stop it now. Helen's mad about you, any fool can see that, and all that's going to happen if you go down this road is that you'll drive yourself mental and ruin a perfectly good weekend away for no reason. Stay clear of Sanne, don't give Aiden Reid airspace in your head, and stop being an idiot, okay?'

Even though the problems between them were far from resolved Phil felt relieved to have his best man back on side. He looked at his watch and then at Simon. 'Hungry?'

'Starving,' said Simon.

'Chinese or Indian?'

'It's your weekend, mate,' said Simon. 'You choose.'

It was just after nine as the Bombay Garden's headwaiter brought over the bill to Phil's table.

'I'll take that,' said Phil, snatching it up. 'It'll be my way of apologising to you lot for ruining the day.'

'No you won't,' said Simon plucking the bill from between his friend's fingers. 'It's mine and let that be the end of it.'

Calling the waiter to one side Simon handled the bill while the rest of the table made ready to leave.

'So what's the plan?' asked Reuben pushing in his chair. 'More beer, different location?'

'There was a place we passed last night that looked quite good,' suggested Spencer. 'It was a couple of doors down from the bar where his Lordship started binge drinking, can't remember the name but I'm sure we'll be able to find it if we keep our eyes open.'

The boys piled out of the curry house into the street, searching for Spencer's mystery pub.

'Are you sure you have to take that bag with you everywhere?' asked Phil as the others broke off leaving him free to talk properly with his dad for the first time that evening. 'Can't you just jam a bottle of tablets into your pockets or something?'

'I can't son,' replied Patrick. 'There's too much of it.'

'You're all right though?' asked Phil. 'You're not sick are you?'

'I'm fine, son,' said Patrick. 'No need to worry about me. I'm indestructible!'

'Even so,' replied Phil. 'Promise me that you'll take it easy tonight, okay?' We've had no major mishaps so far and I'd like to keep it that way.'

'Of course I will,' said Patrick rolling his eyes in dismay. 'Not that I need you telling me what to do. I'm a grown man!'

'I know you are,' said Phil. 'I'm not trying to tell you what to do, Dad, I just want you to look after yourself.'

'Well, if we're all doling out the advice,' countered Patrick, 'might I suggest that you do the same? Getting into rows with your mates, getting us thrown out of paintballing . . . drinking so much you can barely remember the night before . . . I'd have to go a long way to beat what you've been up to this last twenty-fours hours.'

'That's different, and you know it.'

'Different how, because it's you and not me? What's going on with you exactly? I've heard bits and pieces but it would be nice if I could hear what the problem is from my own son.'

'Look, Dad,' said Phil trying and failing to remain patient, 'can we just drop it? It's all sorted now, so there's no point in going over it again is there?'

'So this bloke off the radio isn't sniffing round your Helen after all?'

Phil sighed. The boys had obviously been talking and figured out more of the story than he had hoped. 'No,' replied Phil, 'he isn't . . . well he is sort of but it's more complicated than that . . .'

'Complicated?' questioned Patrick. 'What's that supposed to mean? Is he after your Helen or not? Because if he is, I don't care who he is, I'll sort him out myself.'

'Cheers Dad. That's good to know.' Phil wondered if there was any point confiding in his dad. 'Look, it's like this: I met a girl last night who it turns out used to be married to Aiden Reid. Anyway, she seemed to think the reason they split up was because he still had a thing for Helen and I had sort of planned to see her tonight to find out more, but Si talked me out of it.'

'Talked you out of it?' said Patrick indignantly. 'Why would you want to be talked out of it? If this woman knows more than you, you should hear what she's got to say because at least then you'll be able to make up your own mind.'

'I don't need my mind to be made up,' protested Phil. 'It is made up. Helen's marrying me next weekend. That's all there is to it.'

'If that really is all there is to it then why don't you find out anyway?' suggested Patrick. 'Honestly, son, sometimes I think your sister was born with more testosterone than you. Just get in there, find out what you want to know and then act accordingly. That's the trouble with your generation. Too much thinking and not enough action.'

Phil wasn't about to let that comment go unchallenged. 'Says the man who spent the last two decades of his working life on the dole.'

'But at least I lived the life!' boasted Patrick. 'At least I've got stories to tell! At least when I'm lying on my deathbed I'll have no regrets.'

'Well you should have if you've got anything close to a conscience,' retorted Phil.

'Oh, you know I don't mean all of that,' said Patrick dismissively. 'I mean the other stuff. The life stuff. You shouldn't get trapped in your own head son. If your gut is telling you to talk to this woman and put your mind at rest then that's what you should do. What have you got to lose?'

12.

Armed with the knowledge gleaned from the folded flyer in his pocket that Sanne wouldn't be coming on stage until ten thirty, Phil continued with the evening as planned. This meant that over the next hour he and the boys roamed Leidseplein drifting from theme bars to real ale pubs in search of good times. Now, they were holed up a bit further out of the neon glare of Leidseplein in a tiny bar sandwiched between a bakery and a travel agent's.

'You want another?' asked Simon noticing Phil's empty glass.

'I can't,' Phil replied. 'I'm off in a sec. Where do you reckon you'll be around midnight?'

Simon shook his head and sighed. 'Are you going where I think you're going?' he asked. 'I thought we agreed it was a bad idea.'

Phil glanced over at his father who was deep into an anecdote about the time he roadied for Pink Floyd during the first leg of their 1972 European tour. 'I just changed my mind, that's all.'

Simon raised an eyebrow in resignation. 'Do you want me to come with?' he asked. 'Bit of moral support?'

'I'll be fine,' he replied. 'Just tell me where you'll be at midnight and I'll meet you there.'

Simon looked over at the boys and asked the question. Deano and Patrick answered simultaneously. Deano's suggestion involved a visit to De Wallen while Patrick seemed entirely focused on getting stoned.

'I'm too old to get stoned,' said Simon, 'and I don't want to watch some miserable economic migrant taking off her kit while her dead eyes scream how much she hates me.' He picked up Reuben's guidebook and made a decision on behalf of the group. 'We'll be in a bar called Hoppe near Spuistraat,' said Simon. 'The Dutch drink there apparently so it can't be that bad.'

Outside Phil took a moment to get his bearings. Although he had been in Amsterdam for less than thirty-six hours, he was beginning to get a feel for the city and without even referring to the map in his back pocket he took a left and headed towards the bright lights at the end of the road, confident that he would know exactly where to go once he reached it.

The Yellow Robot, as Phil discovered, was a small subterranean club less than a hundred metres away from Amsterdam's infamous Melkweg club and housed in what according to a sign outside the venue used to be a coffee merchant's back in the 1800s. Relieved to have found the place with relative ease Phil descended the stairs, paid the entrance fee, and then entered the room where a young man on stage armed only with an acoustic guitar was in the middle of what Phil assumed was an ironic cover of a Kanye West song.

The song finished, the crowd clapped and Phil looked around. Although there were plenty of tables dotted about, they were all taken and even standing room at the back of the room appeared to be at something of a premium. Phil made his way to the bar and ordered a beer while the Kanye West cover guy announced in English that he was about to play his final song of the night, a ballad, about a girl he'd once spent the night with during the year that he was living in Barcelona. The audience clearly loved both him and his tragic demeanour and applauded him frantically and later (at his encouragement) even joined in with the song's heartbreaking refrain.

Although Phil loved talking about hi-fi and hi-fi related equipment because of what he did for a living, he had pretty much given up on modern music only stooping to purchase the occasional must-have CD which he would play for a week before abandoning it in favour of stuff that had long since proved its worth and stood the test of time like early Dylan, the Rolling Stones, Etta James, early Don Cherry or even mid-period Beastie Boys. Hearing the Kanye West cover guy, and more importantly seeing the way the audience reacted to him, made Phil resolve that first thing Monday morning he was going to trawl Amazon in a bid to catch up on everything he'd been missing out on since he'd unofficially decided to allow himself to get old.

The house lights came up signalling an interval and Phil sipped on a bottled Amstel while a technician came on stage and began setting up for Sanne, carrying off the previous act's microphone and returning with a new microphone, a stool and a small table on which he placed a bottle of water.

A short while later the house lights went down for a second time and the stage was plunged into darkness as over the PA came the opening bars to Stevie Wonder's 'Isn't She Lovely?' One by one the audience got the joke and a wave of anticipation spread over the crowd. They broke into applause as a single spotlight picked out the chair at the centre of the stage and moments later Sanne, wearing a silky blue dress and green shoes walked on to the stage carrying an acoustic guitar.

Revealing a hitherto unseen sense of comic timing Sanne whispered into the microphone, 'I am, aren't I?' As the Motown soul legend's vocals began the music faded, she strapped on her guitar and plugged it into the amp at her feet, and sitting down on the stool began her opening song, a passionate ballad sung in English, called (if the song's chorus was anything to go by) 'What chance did we have?'

Some three songs into Sanne's set, at least three quarters of the men in the room currently captivated by her every sound or movement had fallen in love with her. Sanne had that kind of face, and she sang those kinds of songs and the killer combination stirred something so instinctive within the masculine frame that had there been any princess-abducting dragons or fair maidens in need of rescuing from the clutches of their evil stepmothers, neither the dragons nor stepmothers would have stood a chance.

Phil wasn't totally immune from this sensation. While he had appreciated Sanne's attractiveness from the moment they met, he had persuaded himself it was a theoretical admiration only. He admired her beauty in the same way that some of his customers admired the new stock in the shop even though they had functioning audio kit at home. A thing of beauty, they would reason, was a thing of beauty whether you actually needed it or not. But here on the stage, singing song after song about love and heartbreak, her intense vulnerability added a depth to Sanne that made her beauty far less abstract because her songs revealed a truth that most in the room could never know first-hand: pretty girls got their hearts broken too.

By the end of her set Phil felt he knew Sanne better than he had previously and as she concluded with a cover of Prince's 'Condition of the Heart' followed by an acoustic rendition of her former band's biggest hit, 'Love Times Two', Phil felt almost as angry with Aiden Reid on her behalf as he did on his own.

When the house lights rose for the final time, Cat Stevens' *Peace Train* began playing over the PA. As he stood staring at the empty stage Phil realised that he hadn't given much thought to how exactly he was going to get to talk to Sanne. Although it was a small club she hadn't been in the audience before the gig and there was every chance that she would leave through some unseen side entrance without him knowing. And while it was true he still had her phone number, the conversation he needed to have would be much more likely face to face.

Finishing off his beer Phil walked up to the technician and asked him if he would mind passing on a message to Sanne. Replying in English the guy refused, informing Phil that he was the fourth guy to have asked in the last ten minutes. He added that even though he personally didn't think she was 'all that' he was pretty sure she wouldn't be interested.

Phil tried to explained that he actually knew Sanne, and that all he wanted was to say hello, but the guy still refused, so then Phil pulled out a fifty Euro note and said, 'Look, just tell her that English Phil from the Van Gogh Museum is here and wants to talk and the money's yours.'

Shrugging, the guy held out his hand for the money up front. Reasoning he wasn't in much of a position to bargain Phil handed over the cash.

'English Phil from the museum?' said the technician, swiftly tucking the money into the front pocket of his jeans.

'No,' corrected Phil. 'English Phil from the *Van Gogh* Museum.'

Offering Phil a 'whatever' shrug the technician jumped on stage and disappeared behind the curtains at the wings. A number of moments passed and just as he was giving up all hope the technician returned with Sanne in tow and from his position at the side of the stage pointed out Phil. Phil waved and she waved back and began walking over to him.

'What are you doing here?' she asked, crouching down. 'I never imagined that you'd really come when you had so much of that oh-so-important drinking to do!'

'Yeah . . . well . . .' he said, trying to pluck up the courage he needed. 'Some things are important.' He took a deep breath and just came out with it: 'I need to talk to you. Quite urgently, actually.'

'Urgently?' Sanne looked confused and understandably so, thought Phil, considering that they barely knew each other. 'Why urgently?'

'Maybe urgent is the wrong word,' corrected Phil. 'Maybe complicated would be better. I promise it shouldn't take more than a few minutes.'

'I'm not sure I can spare the time,' she replied. 'I promised some friends I'd catch up with them later tonight.' She remembered her earlier white lie. 'And this time these friends are real.'

'Look,' replied Phil, 'I can see I'm making you nervous and that's the last thing I want. Let's just have a quick drink here, I'll explain and you can be off with your friends before you know it.'

Sanne considered his proposition carefully. 'You're not a weirdo are you? You didn't seem like one when I first met you but it's hard to tell sometimes!'

'Listen,' he replied, 'by the time I've told you what I need to say you'll definitely think I'm odd but not weird, I promise you.'

Sanne nodded as if to say she had concluded her extensive 'weirdo' detection tests and was analysing the results. 'I can't imagine that you're any weirder than some of the guys who used to follow the band back in the day. Just wait there while I get the promoter to look after my things and we'll go somewhere quieter.'

Sanne turned to walk off stage but then a couple of guys who had been lingering behind Phil clearly trying to overhear their conversation called her over, waving their pens in the air. The look of reverence on their faces as Sanne scribbled her name on the CD covers they had brought along with them was striking, and as soon as she was done they tried to engage her in conversation and when that failed they pulled out their digital cameras and practically begged for a photo session.

When Sanne finally got away Phil was left trading stares with Sanne's fans who were clearly wondering who was the guy in the black suit and tie. Keen to make himself less conspicuous, Phil's eyes fell on Sanne's merchandise stall, which had previously been hidden from view by the audience.

There were a number of CDs, badges, three T-shirts with different designs and a DVD of a recent live show. Phil picked up two CDs one of which was an official looking release called *Late night lullabies* and another that had a deliberately amateurish cover that was entitled *Home Demos 2*. Phil pulled out some money and handed it to the girl who was manning the stall. She carefully wrapped the CDs in a brown paper bag and handed them back as though acknowledging how fastidious Sanne's fans could be about packaging. Phil dropped them into his jacket pocket and returned to the stage to wait for Sanne.

He didn't have to wait long. Within a few minutes she appeared at the side of the stage wearing a denim jacket and, much to the annoyance of the small group of fans who had been staring daggers at him, beckoned him over. Phil followed her as she led him through the semi-darkness of the backstage area down some stairs, along a corridor and out through a fire door into the bustling side street.

Sanne walked as if she had a destination in mind and Phil offered no opposition.

'You were amazing tonight,' said Phil as they walked past a couple of shops selling everything from books to designer chairs. 'Really impressive.'

'Thank you,' she replied. 'They were a good crowd. Amsterdam crowds can sometimes be a little stiff but these guys were great. They were really into it.'

'It was hard not to notice,' said Phil. 'Are your fans always that keen?'

Sanne grinned. 'You mean the guys that wanted the autographs? They're a little intense but they're harmless enough.'

'Were they fans of your old band?'

Sanne shook her head. 'So you know about my old band?' she said. 'How did you guess?'

Phil laughed. 'You played one of their songs.'

'I wouldn't have had you down as a Misty Mondays fan.'

'I wasn't,' replied Phil. 'I just put two and two together, that's all. Don't you like people knowing?'

Sanne shook her head. 'I don't like people thinking they know me just because they've seen things in the papers. That period of my life is over, it was fun while it lasted but it's definitely over.' Sanne came to a halt in front of a dimly lit pub that didn't appear to have a name and was so small it looked more like someone's living room.

'It's not the coolest place in the world,' said Sanne reading Phil's face, 'but I think you'll like it. It's homely . . . like you.'

The barman waved at Sanne the moment she entered the room as did a number of the regulars. As they looked around for a table, a couple at a table in the window stood up and left and Sanne immediately took their table while Phil ordered a white wine and a beer at the bar.

'So,' began Sanne as they clinked glasses, 'what exactly is on your mind?'

'Everything,' replied Phil, though to his ears it sounded more than a little cheesy.

'Everything how?'

Phil struggled to find the right words. 'You and me . . . we're . . . connected.'

Sanne's brow furrowed. 'Is this to do with my old band?'

Phil shook his head. 'That's not the connection. Aiden's the connection,' he swallowed hard. 'Aiden Reid.'

13.

'What's going on?' demanded Sanne, her face lined in fury. 'Are you a journalist?'

'Of course not,' protested Phil. 'I'm just a bloke on his stag weekend!'

'Then why the talk about my ex-husband?' she snapped. 'What's he done now that's made him so newsworthy all of a sudden? I'm sick and tired of you guys following me around and hassling me about him, always taking pictures and poking your noses in where they're not wanted! That's the main reason I left the UK. I don't like you guys in my life!' She picked up her glass and tossed the contents in Phil's face. 'Just leave me alone! Just leave me be or I swear you'll regret it!'

She grabbed her jacket and turned to leave. Desperate to persuade her to stay, Phil made a grab for Sanne's arm. Of all the wrong moves he could have made this was undoubtedly the worst. Not only did it thoroughly enrage Sanne, but every man in the bar too and before he knew it he was being pinned against the wall.

'You've got it all wrong!' yelled Phil over the fracas even though he could no longer see if Sanne was still in the room. 'You've got it all wrong! I'm not a journalist! I'm Helen Richards' boyfriend! You know, Helen Richards as in Aiden's—' Phil stopped as Sanne's face appeared among those already crowded around his own. She shouted something in Dutch to the men and gradually the less aggressive of the pack released their grip on Phil until only one, a young guy wearing a baseball cap and logoed sportswear, remained. Sanne placed her hand on the man's forearm and calmly repeated the phrase that she had told the others until he released Phil's shirt, offering a barely perceptible nod in her direction before returning to the bar where he had been standing with his friends.

Sanne slipped on her jacket, dug deep inside her bag and withdrew her purse. She spoke to the barman in Dutch and gave him a handful of notes. The barman took the cash; Sanne grabbed Phil's hand and dragged him outside.

'Are you all right?' she asked, checking his face for signs of injury. 'They didn't hit you did they?'

'I'm fine,' said Phil, wiping the remnants of Sanne's wine from his face. 'It was nothing.'

Sanne smiled. 'Not even a flesh wound?'

'No.' Phil noticed that he was still holding her hand and pulled it away. 'Not even a flesh wound.'

Sanne began walking. 'I'm sorry about what happened back there. When you mentioned Aiden's name I just saw red and assumed you were a journalist.'

Phil smiled. 'I take it you're not a fan?'

'Hardly,' she replied. 'It was bad enough when I was

in the band, we'd check into hotels and find them waiting outside our bedrooms or one time actually in our bedrooms hiding inside a wardrobe but the minute I started seeing Aiden it went insane. The paparazzi were camped outside the entrance to my apartment morning, noon and night. I couldn't even go to my grandfather's grave in Golders Green without at least one of them following me and taking a snap that would end up under some horrible intrusive headline. It was a living nightmare and not one I'll ever go back to.'

'Helen had that too for a while,' said Phil as Sanne took a sharp left off the main road down a long narrow street, 'obviously nowhere near as bad as you but bad enough. It started when Aiden first got famous so the tabloids started trawling through his friends and family to see if they could get any dirt on him, then when you guys got engaged it took off big time and they offered Helen silly money if she'd agree to dish the dirt in an exclusive. They got so desperate they even tried to drag me into it a couple of times, door-stepping me at work and trying to rile me so that they could get some kind of quote from the bloke going out with Aiden Reid's first love.' Phil winced as a look of hurt flashed across Sanne's features. He would have apologised but thought that it would make things worse. They continued in silence across canal bridges and along tiny cobbled streets until they came to a halt outside a bustling canalside café and took a seat at one of the outdoor tables.

A waitress handed them both menus. Phil looked at

his watch. It was only ten minutes to midnight. If he jumped on a tram now he could be with the boys before they moved on. But even as he constructed his getaway in his head Phil knew that he wouldn't be going anywhere too soon. There was too much to say, too much to talk about.

Tired of lager and desperate to counter the fatigue currently leeching away at his bones Phil ordered an Americano for himself and a cappuccino for Sanne and for good luck added a slice of cheesecake to the order.

As they waited Sanne, obviously keen to avoid any real conversation while they were still in danger of being interrupted by the waitress, told him the history of the area in which they were sitting, how in the seventeenth and eighteenth centuries the city's richest families had built homes there resulting in some of the unique style of architecture throughout the city. As Sanne spoke Phil gazed up at the illuminated three-storey buildings around them and marvelled at one in particular with a turreted roof and stone cornicing elaborately carved into the shape of herds of wild horses. It was truly spectacular and increased his sense of wonderment at the city that for two days had been his home.

The drinks and cheesecake arrived. Phil offered Sanne the first taste of his dessert but she declined. A long silence fell.

'When did you realise who I was?' asked Sanne eventually. 'In the queue when we met or later?'

Phil swallowed down a mouthful of cheesecake. 'I thought you looked familiar the minute I saw you,' he replied, 'but it was when I left the bar that it hit me.'

Sanne picked up Phil's fork and dipped it into the cheesecake. 'So why didn't you say anything when we met at the museum?' She manoeuvred the fork to her lips. 'Were you trying to catch me out or something?'

'It would've been too weird,' replied Phil as she set the fork down on his plate. 'I mean what are the chances? Me meeting you, and us having this huge thing in common?'

'You'd be surprised,' said Sanne. 'My mum once flew out to see me in LA and on the way back who should she sit next to but a woman she used to be best friends with in kleuterschool. They hadn't seen each other since they were six! Weird stuff happens all the time.'

'Maybe,' said Phil. He sighed and took a sip of his Americano. 'But it still felt too odd for my liking.'

'So what changed your mind?' she asked. 'Or is that a silly question?'

Phil's whole frame filled with embarrassment. What exactly had he hoped to learn by talking to Sanne about her ex-husband? Was he simply looking for a way to torture himself for no good reason? 'I was fine until you told me why your marriage broke down . . . and I guess . . . well I guess it sort of freaked me out. I mean your ex is a rich guy and I know from the papers that your divorce cost him big time and the idea that a guy like him would give up half his fortune because he thought he was still in love with my girlfriend was . . .'

'Unsettling?'

'That's it exactly,' said Phil. 'I know it's been a while since you guys split up but do you know if he ever tried to get back in contact with Helen?'

Sanne frowned. 'Don't you think she would tell you if he had?'

Phil shrugged. 'I don't know. Would you have done if you were in her shoes? He's Aiden Reid, if anyone's going to make a bloke feel a bit emasculated it would be someone like him with all his money and fame. Why would you put someone you loved through that? I know Helen inside out. I know what makes her laugh and I know what makes her cry. And if she did hold back the fact that he had been in touch it would be for a good reason.'

Sanne nodded thoughtfully. 'She sounds like a good woman.'

'She is,' replied Phil. 'The best.'

Sanne blinked several times and then rubbed her eyes and Phil knew that he had inadvertently hit a nerve. 'I used to hate her you know.' She looked at Phil, gauging his reaction. 'I used to hate her with every fibre of my being. When I moved in with Aiden I came across some photographs of her tucked away in a box in his wardrobe and I knew that she was someone special. Men like Aiden don't keep photos of women they've been with, at least not these kinds of photos – happy photos, full of warmth and love. I asked him who she was and he just took the photos and told me to mind my own business.'

Phil was confused. 'So he never told you about her?'

'Oh, he told me all right,' said Sanne, 'but it was months later and he was drunk and distraught because his mum was ill at the time and he wasn't coping very well.'

'And what did he say exactly?'

'He told me she was his ex, and that they'd planned to marry but he had been unfaithful to her.'

'And that's all?'

'No,' said Sanne, 'he also told me that he had never stopped loving her.'

Phil felt a rush of blood to his head. 'He actually said that?'

Sanne nodded. 'It's typical Aiden, always wanting what he can't have. It's how he's built.'

'So how did you end up getting married if you knew he felt this way?'

Sanne shrugged philosophically. 'How does anything happen in these situations? You simply become blind to what you don't want to see. By this time I was so in love with him he could have told me anything and it wouldn't have made the slightest difference to how I felt. I adored him. He made me feel like I'd never felt before. That he had these feelings for someone in the past was hurtful, yes, but it was by no means a deal-breaker. I was convinced that if I loved him enough, one day he'd feel that same way about me.'

'And did it work?' he asked, before the full implication of his question reached his brain.

Sanne didn't reply. She pulled a handful of notes from

her purse, tucked them underneath her cappuccino cup and stood up. 'I need to walk,' she said. 'You can come or you can go, it's up to you.'

Berating himself for not having kept his big mouth shut, Phil ran after her and caught her halfway down the cobbled street.

'Listen, Sanne I'm sorry,' he said quickly. 'That question has got to be the stupidest thing I've ever said. I'm an idiot. Just ignore me.'

Sanne wiped her eyes but even without a street light Phil could see her lashes glistening in the moonlight. 'I just find . . . I don't know . . . even now it still hurts a little.' Reaching into her bag she took out her phone, dialled a number, turned to Phil and said: 'How do you feel about—?' but then stopped as her call was answered and she began talking animatedly in her mother tongue. 'That was my friend Janneke,' she explained as she ended the call, 'the friend who I was meeting tonight. She's at her place now with a few of our friends. It's not far from here if you fancy it for a while. They're good people. You'll like them.'

Sanne's friends' small gathering turned out to be a party on the top floors of an old four-storey house with huge windows that looked out across the Amstel. Armed with a can of lager Phil spent the first half-hour touring the house and the second being introduced to Sanne's friends the names of whom had all pretty much eluded him the moment he shook their hands.

Unlike his friends back home in Nottingham (most of

whom worked in ordinary occupations with needlessly complicated job titles) virtually all of Sanne's friends appeared to be 'creative' in some way. Phil had never met so many people who claimed to work in the field of performance poetry, and after the fifth he longed to talk to someone ordinary about something ordinary, if only for a short while.

A tall skinny girl with bright red bobbed hair came over to the performance poet Phil had been stuck with for the last ten minutes, and seizing his opportunity to flee Phil made his way over to Sanne who was on the fringes of a large group standing by the window.

'Are you okay?' she asked as Phil appeared by her side. 'Still enjoying yourself?'

'I'm fine,' said Phil, 'I think the fatigue's just kicking in, that's all.'

'Do you want to get off? I don't mind.'

'No,' said Phil. 'But I tell you what I could do with though . . . your phone, just for a minute, if that's okay.'

'Yeah, of course,' replied Sanne. 'If you want to call your friends and invite them over they'd be more than welcome.'

'I couldn't even if I wanted to,' explained Phil. 'For reasons that I won't go into we all left our phones back in the UK and I've been wanting to call Helen but can't remember her number.'

'So you're going to call a friend and get it?'

Phil shook his head. 'The only person I can think of is my sister who's actually with Helen this weekend and I can't remember her number either.'

'So what are you going to do?'

'Well, if it's okay with you I'll check my voicemail and see if she's called me. I just want to know if she's okay, does that make any sense?'

'Of course,' said Sanne, 'I think it's sweet.'

Sanne explained how to use the phone and then excused herself to go to the kitchen to get them a couple of fresh lagers. Phil, desperate to get away from the noise, headed out into the hallway and began dialling.

The message had been left Friday evening:

Hey you, it's just me saying a quick hello. Arrived safely, the hotel is amazing, and the girls are all here now and we're having a lot of fun. Obviously I'm not looking to cramp your style in front of the boys but I thought you might like to know that I love you madly! No need to ring me back, okay? Love you, bye.

It was so good just to hear her voice and Phil felt comforted. Everything was all right. All of that worrying was for nothing. Aiden Reid was nowhere to be seen. Relieved, he pushed on to hear the second and final message left only an hour earlier:

Phil, it's me. I'm not looking to cause trouble, I promise you, but you know that Aiden Reid guy off the radio? Well he's here at the hotel and Helen knows him – they used to work together or something – and well I don't know how to say this nicely because I know it'll be painful so I'll just come out with it: I've got a horrible feeling that something's going on between the two of them. Ring me when you get this and let me know what you want me to do. Take care and I'll speak to you soon.

14.

Phil had been halfway to the front door when Sanne, carrying the two bottles of lager, had called his name.

'Where are you going?'

'I've left your phone with one of your friends,' explained Phil urgently. 'I have to go.'

Sanne's brow furrowed. 'Go?' she asked, stunned. 'Why? Has someone upset you? Who was it? Let me at least try and sort it out. Please, let me at least try. I'd hate you to just go like this.'

'It's Aiden,' explained Phil. 'When I was checking my messages I found one from my sister. She thinks that something is going on between Helen and Aiden.'

'Why would she say that?' questioned Sanne. 'How would she even know something like that?'

'The girls – Helen and her mates – they've gone to some posh hotel in the Peak District,' replied Phil. 'Caitlin says that Aiden's there too.' He looked at Sanne. 'Now how's that for the king of coincidences?'

Sanne bit her lip. 'Nothing about this sounds right,' she said putting a reassuring hand on Phil's arm. 'I'm not calling your sister a liar but are you sure that she couldn't be mistaken?'

'Mistaken?' replied Phil. 'Mistaken how? I've never even mentioned to Caitlin that Helen knew Aiden so why would she bring his name up now?'

'I don't know . . .' said Sanne. 'Maybe she Googled Helen's name one time and Aiden's name came up?'

'And so she thought she'd ruin my stag weekend with a practical joke?'

'No, of course I'm not saying that but maybe . . . I don't know . . . maybe Aiden was there by accident – he used to take me to those kinds of places all the time when we were together – maybe they spoke and your sister's got a bit freaked out that her sister-in-law to be is on such good terms with someone as famous as Aiden.'

'I'm not naïve,' said Phil, trying his best to stay calm, 'One thing my sister isn't, is stupid. If she's called me at what . . . one in the morning UK time? To tell me she thinks there's something going on between Helen and Aiden it's because she genuinely thinks there is.'

'So what's your plan?'

'Go back to the hotel to get my stuff and then the first flight back home to sort this out face to face.'

'Why don't you just call her first? I'm sure with a bit of detective work you could find out the number of the hotel, call her room and speak to her.'

Phil was aware that Sanne was trying to calm him down but he didn't want to be calmed down. He wanted to take action. Action was the only thing that made sense to him right now. 'What if she's not there?' he said urgently. 'What if he picks up the phone? Look, this is driving me crazy and I haven't even spoken to her. I need to be able to see her, I need her to tell me whatever it is she's got to tell me face to face. Once I see her face, once I look into her eyes, I'll know everything I need to know.' Sanne took Phil by the arm, led him to the stairs and sat him down.

She gripped his hands tightly. 'Listen, before you do anything rash let me just try one thing. I'm still not convinced Aiden is there. Like you say, it would be too much of a coincidence for him to be there by accident, so why don't you let me make a few calls to some people I know back in England who might be able to shed some light on this and then we'll take it from there. What do you say?'

As unsettling as Caitlin's call had been, it did seem a bit far-fetched that Aiden should just happen to be at the same hotel as Helen. And despite the shadow that Aiden had cast over his own relationship did he really believe that Helen would give up on the life they had built together after a single weekend? Like Sanne said, maybe it made sense to see what light she could shed on the matter before he jumped on a plane and headed back to England all guns blazing.

Sanne disappeared back to the party to get her phone while Phil headed downstairs and waited outside staring across the shifting surface of the Amstel as it scattered the moon's reflection into a million tiny fragments. It was hard not to appreciate the city's beauty. And as he stood watching a passing boat filled with revellers he imagined how if Helen had been here to share the view it might have become one of those moments that they would always remember, like the time they had driven through the night to Southwold to watch the sunrise over the north sea, or the time a few years later when they had got snowed in at Helen's mum's cottage and had spent a morning lying in bed watching the snow fall past the bedroom window. Without her by his side, it was just another one of the stream of passing minutes that made up the hours of his waking day.

The sound of footsteps alerted Phil to Sanne's descent. He studied Sanne's face and knew immediately that his fears had been confirmed.

Sanne made her way out of the front door with Phil following close behind.

'The Royal Park Hotel is not too far from here,' she explained keeping her eyes focused on the road ahead. 'We can get a cab from there to your hotel, pick up your things and drive . . .' Her voice choked. '. . . drive to the airport.'

Phil put a hand on her shoulder. 'Are you okay?'

Sanne shook her head and wiped away tears. 'My mother is a staunch dyed in the wool Catholic and when my sister and I were kids we were always screaming how much we hated each other and whenever we did this she would always take us to one side and tell us how wrong it was to hate another human being. But right now, I don't think there's any other word for how I feel about Aiden.' Phil felt the muscles in his stomach tighten as he braced himself for the blow. 'Your sister was right.'

'About Aiden being at Helen's hotel?'

Sanne nodded. 'Have you heard of Ally Fallon?' Phil nodded. She was the flame-haired former kids' TV presenter, a real party girl who was always in the tabloids, falling out of some bar on the arm of some long-haired tattooed musician. 'Well Ally and I go way back to when we were at stage school together, and now she's engaged to Karl Peters.' Phil nodded again: Karl Peters was the Five Live guy notorious for shouting at the guests on his show to get his point across. 'So I called Ally because Karl is one of Aiden's closest friends and I asked her if she knew where Aiden was this weekend and the moment I said his name, I just sensed that something was up, and well, after that she told me everything. Apparently Aiden turned up at their house in the early hours last weekend and he was drunk and maudlin but wouldn't say why, and eventually Karl managed to coax out of him what the problem was: he'd just heard from a friend of a friend that you and Helen were getting married the weekend after next and it had sent him over the edge. So anyway, Karl sits up with Aiden all night and by the morning they've come up with a plan for him to get Helen back.'

'Which was?'

'To find out where Helen was having her hen night, crash it by inventing a good reason to be at the venue and then somehow talk her into taking him back. By the Monday morning they had found out the hotel, by the Tuesday they had roped in a few of Aiden's celebrity mates to come along in the hope that they might impress either Helen or her friends and by the Wednesday it had been decided the cover story would be that Aiden and his friends were there for Karl's stag weekend.'

Phil felt as if his head was about to explode and rubbed it frantically trying to calm down his overactive synapses. Was this really happening? Had some bloke off the telly really recruited a bunch of his celebrity mates in a bid to try and seduce Phil's fiancée? None of it seemed real. He needed more information.

'And that's it? That's everything?'

Sanne nodded. 'That's it.'

'And your friend didn't say anything about Helen or whether Aiden's plan was working?'

'No. She hasn't spoken to Karl since Friday night.'

'So why did you look so horrified when you came to tell me? I get that this guy has gone to a lot of effort but there's something else you're not telling me, I can feel it. It's almost as if you think I don't stand a chance.'

'Of course, it's not like that. That was just me overreacting. It was a shock, that's all.'

Phil remained unconvinced. 'I'm not taking another step until you tell me exactly why you were so worried. I need to know.'

Sanne took a deep breath. 'Because I know what he's like. Aiden is a man who spends all day every day charming hundreds of thousands of people of all ages and races, rich or poor into listening to him day, after day, after day. People love him. People love him because they think he's warm and funny and honest and all the things they know they'll never be. But most of all people love him because even though they know it's not true, when they hear his voice coming to them through the airwaves, they feel like he's actually talking to them and them alone. Now imagine how it must feel when he really is talking to you and you alone. I don't know Helen, but I do know Aiden and I know that when he wants something – whether it's the most coveted job in UK radio or one of thirty-six super rare classic Italian sports cars that he knows he'll get bored of within a week – there's nothing he won't do to get it. Because for men like Aiden it's the getting, not the having, that makes them feel alive.'

The taxi pulled up in front of the hotel. Phil climbed out of the car and Sanne instructed the driver to wait.

Sanne said she'd wait in the lobby and took a seat next to a fake potted palm as Phil made his way up to the second floor. Phil barely registered the state of his room as he frantically packed his case. Whether it was his mud-sodden tracksuit or his dirty underwear, or the CDs of Sanne that he had bought earlier in the night, it all got shoved in until all his belongings were packed away, and his passport placed carefully in the inside pocket of his jacket.

As he made his way downstairs he wondered if the boys were back and whether he should check to see if they were in their rooms but even as this thought occurred to him he dismissed it. This was the last night of probably one of the last stag dos any of them would be going on for quite a long time; none of his friends (still less his father) would be getting in any time soon.

He handed over his key card to the girl in reception, gave her his room number and crossed his fingers that room service hadn't come across the pneumatic drill hidden in the wardrobe.

The girl tapped away on the keyboard in front of her and stared at the screen. 'I've got a note here that we've taken a message for you.'

She walked over to a bank of drawers, opened one and began flicking through the drop files in front of her. Phil willed her to find it quickly. It was from Helen. It had to be. She must have called his room and when he hadn't answered thought it best to leave a message on reception. She must want to tell him about Aiden, he reasoned, she must want to tell him that everything was going to be fine.

The girl stood up, holding the piece of paper aloft. 'Finally!' She handed him the note. On it was written the date and the time (some two hours earlier) and a message requesting that he call the number that had been written down below. Phil didn't recognise the number. It wasn't Helen's mobile number, in fact it didn't even look like an English number.

Phil settled the bill and returned to the lobby. Sanne was playing with her phone.

'I was just texting Ally thanking her for being so nice to me on the phone. I didn't appreciate how late it was when I called her. She was probably still up partying with her friends, but even so, I feel a bit bad. All done?'

Phil shook his head. 'Not quite. I was just checking out when I got this.' He handed the note to Sanne. 'It looks like a Dutch number to me.'

'It is,' said Sanne. 'Do you want me to call it?'

Phil shook his head. 'I'm sure it's nothing.'

Sanne smiled. 'Then use my phone and I'll go check on the driver.'

Phil dialled the number and waited. It rang three times and a voice, clearly a recording, started speaking to him in Dutch. He could tell he was being offered options of the 'press 1 for Yes, press 2 for No' variety, but had no idea what exactly those options were. He ended the call. Someone must have made a mistake.

He walked through the lobby to the front entrance and found Sanne arguing with the cab driver. The cab driver seemed more amused than annoyed by Sanne's tirade but once she had finished he simply shrugged, gave her the middle finger and drove off.

'What was the problem there?'

'The man was a pig! We don't need him, there are plenty of taxis in Amsterdam at this time of night.' She exhaled heavily and ran her fingers through her hair. 'Did you find out who the message was from?'

'No, it was a recorded voice speaking in Dutch. Didn't make any sense. I think maybe the hotel made a mistake.'

Sanne took her phone from Phil's hand, pressed redial and put the phone up to her ear. Phil watched intrigued as she followed the instructions, punched in the correct numbers before finally getting to speak to a real live person.

The conversation took place in Dutch. Several times Phil saw her looking over at him until finally she ended the call.

'So, what's the deal? Wrong number?'

Sanne's brow furrowed. 'Is your father here with you on your stag do?'

Phil nodded. 'What's that got to do with the call?'

'Well that was the police,' she replied, 'apparently he's managed to get himself arrested.'

15.

It was a quarter past two as a tired and weary Phil, together with Sanne entered Bureau Beursstraat in De Wallen in the heart of the red-light district. A sole police officer manned the front desk hidden behind a plexiglass screen and was taking details in English from a young Spanish woman and her boyfriend. The woman had apparently just had her bag stolen by two youths on a motor scooter and was particularly upset because the bag contained her passport.

Phil felt sorry for the young woman but even more sorry for himself. He should have been on his way to the airport and this diversion was turning what was already a terrible situation into a catastrophe. Every minute that passed was another minute that Aiden Reid would be using to change Helen's mind. Phil had seriously considered leaving his father where he was and letting him sort out his own problem but he would never forgive himself if anything bad happened.

It took twenty minutes for the duty officer to deal with the Spanish couple but then as Phil stepped forward he muttered in Dutch that Sanne translated saying he would be back in a minute.

Phil's irritation at the delay was obvious, and picking up on this Sanne gently nudged him aside as the officer returned. She spoke in Dutch and they talked for ages, occasionally breaking into laughter. Even without a rudimentary knowledge of the language Phil could tell that she was flirting and that somewhere during the course of the conversation the officer had recognised her and had been flattered that she was being so nice to him.

Finally, the officer grinned and pointed to a row of grey plastic chairs.

'We should take a seat,' said Sanne as the police officer disappeared out of view. She sat down on one of the chairs. Phil didn't want to sit, he was too wired with nervous energy to find any comfort from taking the weight off his feet but Sanne had asked to and he felt he couldn't say no when she was doing so much for him.

'Well, the good news is that he should be out by first thing in the morning,' said Sanne.

'And the bad?'

'He's been arrested for dealing drugs.'

'Dealing drugs!' Phil couldn't believe what he was hearing. 'My dad's a bit of a liability but I'm pretty sure he's not a drug dealer. This makes no sense at all! And while I'm at it where were the boys? Why weren't they looking out for him?'

'According to the officer they were doing a sweep in De Wallen after some complaints about dealers hassling tourists when they caught your father in the act of selling a hash cake to an American tourist. On arresting him they discovered that he had a further twenty-nine carefully tucked away in his rucksack.'

'He told me that bag of his was for his heart medication! I wondered why he'd been carrying that damn thing round with him all weekend.'

'But where did he get them from? No coffee shop would sell them in bulk like that.'

Phil shook his head as an answer slowly dawned on him. 'He made them.'

'Who? Your father?'

Phil nodded. 'That's my dad all over. He's the only man in the world who would buy cannabis in the UK, take it through customs and then try and sell it in one of the few places in the world where it's freely available.' Phil stood up, every muscle riddled with fatigue. 'Well now that little mystery is cleared up at least we can go.'

'Not yet, I talked the duty officer into asking his boss if it might be okay for you to see him.'

Phil checked his watch. 'I don't want to see him and I certainly don't want to see him now when I should be at the airport. He's okay, and while the daft old sod might not appreciate being locked up I can't imagine that it will do him any harm.'

'Fine,' said Sanne flatly, 'we'll go if that's what you want.'

She rose to her feet and Phil bent down to pick up his bag but then the sound of the duty officer returning to his desk made them both turn around.

'You can come now,' the officer called out to them in English. 'He's in interview room two.'

The officer pressed a buzzer and a reinforced metal door to the left of them clicked open. Phil followed Sanne through the door, along a corridor and into the interview room where Patrick was sitting on a chair behind a plain grey table.

As annoyed as Phil was, he couldn't help but feel sympathy for his father. With an officer standing behind him he looked small and old.

'You okay, Dad?'

'Never better, son. I've been in a few nicks in my time but I must say the Dutch ones are easily in my top three.' He looked over at Sanne. 'Who's your friend?' Phil made the introductions. 'Pleased to meet you, Sanne, although it would have been much nicer under different circumstances.'

'Look, Dad, Sanne's had a word with the duty officer and he says you'll be free to go first thing in the morning. There may be a fine but I'll sort that out now.'

'And you'll pick me up in the morning?'

Phil shook his head. 'No Dad, I can't. I'm heading back home now. There's sort of an emergency – a work thing – it needs my attention straight away. I'll leave a message at the hotel for the boys to come and get you. Where are they by the way? Did you lose them?'

Phil's dad winked. 'I'll tell you later son, you take care and I hope you get things sorted.' He looked at Sanne. 'Oh, and nice to meet you love, sorry it's been so short but maybe I'll see you at the wedding next weekend. In my experience someone always drops out at the last minute so there'll be plenty of room for you if you want to pop over.'

Sanne grinned to cover her embarrassment and then they said their goodbyes and left the room.

'I'm going to go and pay the fine,' said Phil quickly in the hope that they might be able to skip any awkward silence.

'I'll wait for you outside.'

Although the fine was large enough to have covered Phil's share of a very nice holiday for two somewhere posh in the Caribbean, he was glad that for the moment at least his dad was out of trouble.

Stepping outside Phil spotted Sanne hailing another cab. She waved to him to join her and they set off to the airport.

Within minutes of leaving the confines of central Amsterdam Sanne had closed her eyes and as the driver seemed absorbed by the phone-in show on his radio Phil was free to let his thoughts roam unchecked.

He was surprised to discover that the main topic on his mind was the woman whose head now rested on his shoulder. Forty-eight hours ago she had been little more than a name in a newspaper and now later they were . . . what exactly? He thought back to the moment in the queue outside the bar when she had smiled at him and told the bouncer that he and the boys were with her and her friends. Then there had been that moment after the Van Gogh Museum when she had wanted to show him Vondlepark; was it his imagination or had there been real disappointment in her eyes when he'd had to go? And tonight at the party she had put her hand on his arm and he had felt as if every nerve ending had been alerted by a single contact. Was this all in his mind? Was he reading too much into it? And what did this mean for the way he felt about Helen?

Phil rubbed his eyes. He didn't want to live in a dream world where beautiful women he barely knew fell in love with him over the course of a manic weekend. He belonged in the real world, the one in which his mates drank pints, his mum cooked Sunday roasts and he fell asleep on the sofa in the arms of the woman that he loved after a long day at work. A momentary fantasy versus a lifetime's reality? It wasn't even a fair fight. Helen was the girl he wanted, he was sure of that. She would always be the one for him.

Phil filled the rest of the journey imagining in great detail the punch he would throw in Aiden Reid's direction the moment he laid eyes on him. One fist jabbed through the air at lightning speed and making such a perfect connection with his nose that Reid would know he'd messed with the wrong man.

Phil didn't care whether it ended with the police being called or pictures of him across every tabloid in the country, all he cared about was kicking seven bells out of Aiden Reid.

Reaching the airport Phil gently roused Sanne and paid the driver before climbing out of the car. He felt oddly calm. Everything was going to be okay. Everything was going to turn out for the best.

The first sign that his initial feelings of well-being might be premature came when he looked at the departure board and saw that that there were no flights in or out of the airport until 5.05 a.m. The second sign came when he realised that there was no one manning any of the low budget airline desks and the KLM desk said the first available flight to the UK that wasn't already fully booked wasn't leaving until seven in the evening, a whole hour after he would have been flying home with the boys anyway.

'And there's no way you can get me there any earlier?'

'Without taking a transfer somewhere else? No, and even then I couldn't guarantee you'd get there any earlier. It's the middle of summer, Mr . . .' she glanced down at his passport that he had handed over during the course of the conversation, . . . Hudson . . . the height of the holiday season, many airports are already at maximum capacity. I'm afraid it's just one of those things.'

Phil barely spoke a word in the cab on the way back into Amsterdam. There wasn't a great deal to be said. If even half of Sanne's claims about Aiden were true, the chances were he would have been too late anyway.

'Do you think she always loved him?'

The question was as much a surprise to Phil as it was to Sanne. She looped her arm through Phil's pulling him closer to her.

'Don't do this to yourself, Phil. It's not worth it.'

'I'm not sure she did,' continued Phil quietly. 'I think . . . I think she really did try her hardest to get over him. You would, wouldn't you, if someone had hurt you like that? You'd make all kinds of promises to yourself not to let them do something like that again. But wouldn't a small part of you always be wondering "what if?" Wouldn't some part of you – a part that you might not want to exist – still be holding out for that happy ending? It's how we're built isn't it? No matter how many times you get slapped in the face you have to believe that next time will be different. And then in comes the guy who hurt you all those years ago, and he wants to make things better and to prove he's not all talk – this time it will be different.' Phil looked out of the window at the bright lights of the passing buildings. 'How could she not fall for that? How could she not think that if she chose him it would finally lift the shadow that he'd cast over her life? All that hurt, all that suffering wouldn't have been for nothing then, would it?' He looked at Sanne. 'If he'd have come back to you like that, would you have taken him back?'

Sanne couldn't meet his eyes.

'It's fine,' he said, reaching across to take her hand, 'it really is, I wouldn't have expected you to answer any other way. Everybody's got an Aiden in their life and I'm pretty sure that in time Helen will become mine.'

The traffic on Herenstraat had been stationary for the best part of twenty minutes. Tired of watching the blue lights of police cars and an ambulance, Sanne paid the driver and climbed out of the car. Unsure of his exact plans Phil climbed out of the car too and joined her on the pavement.

'What are you going to do?'

Sanne yawned. 'I'll walk home from here. My place is the other side of town but it shouldn't take too long.'

'You can't walk on your own at this time of night. Let me take you home. I'm pretty sure that I've got the hang of this place so I won't get lost when I head back to the hotel.'

'Have you forgotten?' grinned Sanne. 'You've already checked out.'

'Then I'll check back in again, or if the worst comes to the worst I'll wake up one of the boys and kip in his room.'

They turned left along Herenstraat heading in the direction of Prisengracht. Apart from the odd cyclist and occasional car, these streets were empty, making it seem like he and Sanne were the last two people on earth.

They were too exhausted to talk and as if to counter the silence at some point their hands reached out for one another in the darkness and formed a union of fingers.

Skilled as he was at avoiding such issues, Phil couldn't manage more than a few moments without wondering exactly where the end of this evening might take him.

They took a left into Egelantiersgracht, a pretty tree-lined street with houses on either side overlooking the central canal, stopping a little way before the first bridge.

'This is my place,' said Sanne, and she reached into her bag for keys.

Phil looked up at the five-storey house, wondering which of the flats belonged to her.

'I'm guessing your place is the top one.'

Sanne shook her head.

'Okay, the next one down.'

She shook her head again.

'The next one?'

She shook her head one last time.

'You own the whole bloody lot?'

Sanne shrugged. 'What can I say? I had a good divorce lawyer.' She pointed to the top of the house. 'The top floor is a sound-proofed studio and I use the bottom floor for my yoga classes or the odd dance class, and I'm always having friends and their kids over to stay but yeah, basically, it's just me and a big old house.'

'I should go,' said Phil quickly. Now that the moment he had been trying not to think about was here it was disconcertingly unreal. 'I'm sure I'll be able to find my way back.'

Sanne held his gaze.

'You don't have to.'

'Maybe not,' he replied, and looked down at his hands that were still entwined with Sanne's, 'but can you think of any way this might be a good idea?'

Sanne shook her head, and still holding his hand she opened up the heavy front door and they stepped inside.

Sunday

16.

Something as simple as a person entering a room can be enough to break the spell between two potential lovers; a new dawn can have a similar effect.

With his arms still wrapped tightly around Sanne's waist Phil had been thinking about this phenomenon as he watched the tiny shards of light breaking through the wooden shutters across Sanne's bedroom illuminating the dust particles in the air and making them appear to dance.

Sanne gently squeezed the hand that had been resting on her belly.

'Are you awake?'

Phil yawned. 'Yeah.'

'Did you sleep well?'

'Okay. You?'

'Not bad, though I can't imagine I'll be good for much today.'

There was a silence. Phil wondered what might be going through Sanne's head. 'I've been thinking,' he began. 'Maybe I will go and pick up my dad. Make sure he's okay and everything.'

'Yeah sure, of course, you should do that.'

'But once I've got him, maybe the three of us could go out for breakfast.'

'That would be great. There are a couple of nice places in Waterlooplein overlooking the Amstel, they aren't too far from where your dad's being held.'

'Sounds great. How long do you think it should take me?'

Sanne shrugged. 'Not long. If I meet you in an hour by the Spinoza statue you should have more than enough time.' Phil swallowed as Sanne wearing nothing but a T-shirt and her underwear, crossed the room and disappeared into the hallway. She really was stunning.

Returning a few moments later with a towel and a toothbrush still in its packet Sanne handed them to him and sat down on the edge of the bed.

'You can use the en-suite to take a shower or there's another bathroom down the hallway.'

Phil picked up the towel. 'I'll use the bathroom down the hallway and leave you in peace for a while.' He looked guiltily at his suit trousers lying on the floor.

'I'm going to make myself a coffee, do you want one?' said Sanne.

Phil interpreted this as code for 'I'm going to give you five minutes to put your trousers on,' and said yes in relief.

Sanne left and he slipped them on. Feeling a sudden heaviness in his heart, Phil lay back on the bed and began to wonder if he wasn't in danger of making the biggest mistake of his life.

Nothing had happened.

Although if he was being totally honest it wasn't for want of trying on his part. It had been Sanne who had saved him from himself. Ready to abandon nine years of loyalty Phil had made every effort to let her know how he felt. After all, he wasn't cheating when he'd already been cheated on was he? But Sanne would have none of it. She wanted to be close to him, but she made it clear that she didn't want to be anyone's cause for regret. And so while certain lines had been crossed, others hadn't even come close to being traversed and, while not even a single kiss had passed between them, the fact that they had awoken partially dressed and wrapped in each other's arms spoke volumes about what they had felt.

Had Phil fallen for Sanne? He considered the question carefully on his way to the bathroom and felt sure that the correct answer must lie somewhere in his head. What he did know for sure was that he had never met anyone like Sanne. She was different, and that difference spoke to Phil in a way that he had never thought possible. Last night had taught him that he could be a completely different person living a completely different life. Did a person exist who had never been tempted by that prospect? He thought about his childhood and the embarrassment he'd felt at having free school dinner tickets, he thought about the tiny house that he had grown up in and the graffiti and the litter that had plagued his estate, he thought about his education and exams he had failed and the opportunities he had missed. With a single action all the worries of his past could belong to another life and another time, and he could concentrate on being someone new somewhere new. It was a pipe dream of course, a holiday state of mind brought on by being free of the day-to-day routine, but what a pipe dream and what a state of mind.

He appeared fully dressed at the kitchen door. The room was modern, tasteful and obviously expensive. Sanne was sitting at a dining table underneath a window looking down at the canal beneath. A mug of coffee was by her hands, a second sat on the table beside her.

'I think I'd better get off.'

'What about the coffee?'

'I'll have to leave it. So, I'll see you later?'

'Eleven, by the Spinoza statue, Waterlooplein.'

'Promise?'

'Promise.'

They hugged goodbye but the embrace felt different, awkward. Phil thought about the shards of light that he had watched coming through the bedroom shutters. Everything looks different in the daytime, her embrace seemed to say, even love.

Beursstraat politiebureau in the daytime was a considerably more hospitable place than it had been in the early hours of Sunday morning. There were two officers manning the duty desk and a much shorter queue, which resulted in Phil's dad arriving more quickly than he had expected.

Patrick still looked old and weary, just as on their

last visit but there was a brightness about his eyes that had been missing before. 'Son, what are you doing here? I thought you had a work emergency?'

'It's fine,' said Phil. 'It's sorted. You all right, Dad?'

'Of course I am,' he turned to the officer who had escorted him into the waiting room. 'Son, this is Peter, he's been looking after me this morning.'

The officer was a tall blond man who couldn't have looked more Dutch if he had been wearing clogs and a PSV Eindhoven top. Phil gave him a nod and raised an eyebrow in sympathy.

'Your father, he's a bit of a character, isn't he?'

'You could say that.'

'He's been regaling us all with stories of his past touring with bands. Did you know, back in 1972 he fell asleep in a hotel room in Amsterdam and woke up in a tree in Vondelpark?'

'I may have heard that story once or twice.'

'Right then, Pat,' said the officer holding out his hand, 'it has been nice meeting you but let's hope that we don't meet again, at least not under these particular circumstances.'

Patrick raised his hands in surrender. 'On that, young Peter, you have my word! My days in the drug trade are over for good.'

The two men shook hands while Phil looked on with a look of bewilderment.

'So where to now?'

Phil looked at his dad. 'This hasn't even slowed you down has it?'

'Not for a second. They haven't built a jail that can keep hold of Patrick Hudson.'

'What were you even doing bringing hash cakes into the country?'

'So you know?'

'Well I couldn't think of any other reason why you'd insist on carrying that stupid rucksack wherever you went. Are you mad? One: if the border police had picked you up with that lot in the UK I can guarantee that they would have been a lot less friendly than Peter here, and two: why would you bring hash cakes into Amsterdam of all places? There's a shop on virtually every street corner selling the stuff!'

'Yeah, but it's the commercial stuff, no one likes that, it's far too strong. My stuff was guaranteed all organic and pesticide free.'

The penny dropped.

'You're growing it?'

Patrick let out a schoolboyish chuckle that managed to be at once charming and annoying. 'I got the basics from the internet in the local library and then filled in the gaps from some books I borrowed off Little Stevie from the pub. I've turned over part of the greenhouse on my allotment to full-time cultivation.'

'You're growing it on the allotment?'

Patrick nodded sheepishly. 'And a bit on the windowsill at home. But I promise you it was for a good cause.'

'And what cause would that be, Dad, the keep Patrick Hudson in beer, fags and horses fund?'

'No,' said Patrick. 'It was for a wedding present for you and Helen. I know you don't think much of me, and it's not like I've been the greatest dad in the world, but I did want to do something to show that I wished you both all the luck in the world.'

'What were you going to get?'

'I don't know, son, do I? A tea set . . . some cutlery . . . something or other from John Lewis in the Victoria Centre if I could scrape together enough cash.'

Phil and never felt guiltier.

'You know you don't have to do any of that. Helen and I have got everything we need.'

'I just wanted to give you something nice, something that might make you think that you old man's not a total dead loss.'

Phil laughed, 'You would've had to sell a lot of hash cakes to get the cash together for a private jet, Dad.'

'Doesn't mean that I couldn't try though, does it?'

Had they been any other father and son, this might have resulted in a man-hug, but as it was they simply exchanged grins, shoved their hands deep into their pockets and kept their eyes fixed on the road ahead.

It was five to eleven by the time Phil reached the Spinoza statue on Waterlooplein, and as he had suspected there was no sign of Sanne. She wouldn't come, he knew that. Last night had been last night and this morning was a whole different story.

Patrick sat down at the base of the statue. 'Who is it we're meeting again?'

'Sanne,' replied Phil, 'you know, the woman you met last night. The one that used to be married to Aidan Reid.'

Patrick considered this. 'So did you get your answer? You know, find out what it was you wanted to know? You were worried about her ex-husband or something.'

Phil shrugged. 'It's hard to say. We talked but I'm not sure I'm any the wiser.'

'But you're not worried about Helen any more, are you? This Aiden Reid guy, he's out of the picture?'

'I don't know, Dad,' said Phil, 'I really don't.'

They waited by the statue for the best part of twenty minutes, talking about the past, making comments about the people they saw and the buildings around them, and it was only when Patrick began to moan that he could murder a cup of tea, that Phil finally accepted that Sanne wasn't going to turn up.

There was a café opposite the statue and although it seemed busy, they headed towards the entrance.

They had barely taken more than a few steps when Phil heard someone calling out his name and turned around to see Sanne, cycling furiously and waving at him as she crossed the bridge. Leaving his father outside the café he ran over to the bridge to meet her.

Sanne came to a halt right in front of him and dismounted. She was wearing a cream T-shirt, a denim skirt and flip-flops and despite having only slept for a handful of hours still managed to look amazing. Phil wished that he had at least changed his shirt, let alone his underwear, and was aware that facially speaking he looked like a man who had had a very rough weekend in Amsterdam.

Phil was glad that he had been wrong about her. He was glad that there was still hope. 'I was beginning to think you weren't going to come.'

Sanne looked directly at him. 'I wasn't.'

Phil nodded, it made sense of course. 'But you're still hungry?'

Sanne grinned. 'Starving.' She glanced back over the bridge. 'There's a little place I go to a lot with friends. It's a bit further down but I think you'll like it. It's a nice Dutch place, no luke-warm tea in chipped mugs, no tomato ketchup in a squeezy bottle and definitely no English breakfasts!'

The café was just as Sanne had described. They found a table outside for three, sat down and perused the menus.

Patrick, being Patrick, opted to stick with what he knew and asked Sanne to order him bacon and eggs but Phil, wanting to both impress Sanne and distance himself from his father's limited outlook on Dutch cuisine selected a dish at random from the Dutch menu called *ontbijtkoek* and seemed thoroughly pleased with himself when he had done so.

Sanne, who had ordered an egg-white omelette on brown toast, looked at him and smiled as the waitress left the table.

'Do you even know what you've ordered?' she asked, clearly amused by his choice.

Phil hoped to bluff his way through. 'Is it some kind of Dutch sausage?'

'It's a cake made from rye flour and spice that comes with butter. I quite like it, and my mother adores it, but I'm pretty sure after the night you've had you'd be better off having something like *Uitsmijter*. It's still Dutch, you'll love it and best of all you still get your "I love the Netherlands Brownie points".'

Sanne called the waitress back and reordered Phil's breakfast for him and once that was done she set about charming Patrick which, with Sanne looking the way she did, took all of ten seconds. It took Patrick approximately three and a half minutes to return the compliment by telling her, without a single deviation in the detail, about how the last time he'd been in Amsterdam he'd gone to sleep in a hotel bedroom and woken up in a tree in Vondelpark.

With the sunshine, the canalside setting and the laughter, it was, thought Phil as he finished the last of his Uitsmijter (fried eggs, ham and aged Gouda on white bread), one of the tastiest meals he had ever eaten and one of the most memorable. But as the waitress appeared to clear away their plates, and his gaze briefly met Sanne's he realised that it was all about to come to an end.

Phil paid the bill, and Sanne suggested that as it was such a beautiful day they should take a stroll along the back up to the edge of De Wallen before she would take her leave.

Pushing Sanne's bike for her, Phil tried to prolong the

journey, eking out precious minutes by asking Sanne about the various buildings that they passed along the way. Finally Sanne came to a halt and explained to Patrick that it was time for her to say goodbye.

Patrick hugged her tightly, 'You're the second Dutch person today that I've really got on with and I'm quickly coming to the conclusion that I like your lot more than I like my own.'

Sanne kissed his cheek. 'What can I say? The feeling's mutual.'

Instructing his father to sit on a nearby bench, Phil walked with Sanne until they were out of his father's eyeline to say his goodbyes but when he opened his mouth he couldn't think of what to say.

'This is ridiculous,' he said eventually. 'It's like my whole mind's gone blank.'

Sanne put her arms around him and held him tightly. 'I should go,' she said finally. She looked up at him, quickly pressed her lips against his own and hugged him tightly. 'I'm not very good at goodbyes.'

Phil kissed the top of her head. 'Look,' he said, 'I am coming back.'

'Don't say that, please, don't say that if you don't absolutely mean it.'

'Why wouldn't I mean it? It's all I've been thinking about since last night.'

'Because you haven't seen Helen. Because you haven't worked things through. Because you don't know anything for sure. And you need to be sure about this, Phil. There's still a chance for you and Helen, all the Aiden stuff might not be as it seems, and then this time next week your life could be as exactly as you've always wanted it to be.'

'But it won't, I just feel it.'

'You need to know for sure.'

'And you'll wait?'

'This isn't about me, it's about Helen. You have to have faith in her. You have to believe the best of her until you know the truth. Despite everything she just might have what it takes to amaze you, and prove you wrong. But you need to fight for her, don't give up until you've explored every possible avenue, proved to her that she's the one for you.'

17.

It was after one as Phil and Patrick reached the hotel lobby and began searching for the boys. On the basis that they would have long since had to check out of their rooms Phil reasoned that even with the good weather there was every chance after the night of drinking they had no doubt indulged in that they wouldn't have gone too far. But when after half an hour of searching the bar, the restaurant and even the hotel toilets proved fruitless, he began to think he would simply have to meet them at the airport.

Frustrated he wondered aloud where could they be, only to have Patrick answer back: 'Any one of a million places. It's not like Amsterdam's Derby city centre is it?'

Phil wasn't convinced. 'Dad, with the best will in the world the boys would be easy to find even if we'd all gone to New York. They're creatures of habit, plus they'll have massive hangovers and be desperate to get rid of them and finally, they probably won't have eaten anything since . . .' Phil stopped as it dawned on him exactly where his friends would be. 'I'm an idiot! I know exactly where they are, right. That place we went to yesterday. They'll be at the Shamrock Inn off Dam

Square knocking back a full English breakfast and wishing for the most part that they were dead.'

Phil was right about everything. Not only were the boys at exactly the same bar, they were even at the same table and when they spotted Phil and Patrick crossing the square they let out a mighty cheer followed by a round of applause.

'Like father like son!' called out Degsy as the two men approached the table. 'Where have you two been all night? Living it up without us? We've been looking for you everywhere.'

'And you thought you'd find us by parking your arses outside an Irish pub and tucking into a double heart-attack on a plate?'

'So where were you then?' asked Simon. 'We stayed in Café Hoppe until gone one waiting for you to turn up.'

Phil shrugged. 'Long story, I'll explain it all later.'

Simon looked at Patrick. 'And what happened to you? One minute we were all in that bar in De Wallen and the next it was like you'd just vanished.'

Phil and his dad exchanged glances. 'I don't know what to say boys. I can only apologise for any trouble that I caused.'

'But where were you? We looked for you for ages.'

Phil knew the boys wouldn't give up until they got their answer. 'He got nicked.'

'Nicked?' said Spencer spitting a mouthful of tea back into his mug, 'What for?'

Phil looked at his dad. 'Do you want to tell them or shall I?'

'It was a bit of a misunderstanding with the local constabulary lads. Nothing to be proud of.'

'He got caught selling hashcakes to tourists.'

This time it was Reuben's turn to spit out his tea. 'He got caught doing what?'

Phil decided to jump in before the questions got out of hand. 'Look, it's all done and dusted and I'm sure, once he's had time to digest it all, he'll bore you to tears next time you see him, but for now, let's just say it's a lesson learned.' Phil checked out the self-inflicted damage that the boys had wreaked about their own person. Degsy's skin looked grey, Reuben had dark shadows under his eyes and Simon's eyes were so bloodshot that they almost looked like they would crack if he blinked too hard. 'I don't need to ask how the rest of your night went, do I? Your faces say it all. What time did you get in?'

Simon shook his head mournfully. 'We didn't. After we lost your dad we went to some club near Leidesplein and when we got bored of that we went to another and then around six some girls that Deano got talking to told us about some bar that they were going to, so then we went there and had a few drinks and Deano didn't get anywhere with the girls, so we pretty much fell asleep on the sofa and by the time we woke up it was gone ten. We staggered out, jumped on a tram to the hotel, had to jump off it because it was going the wrong way, jumped on a different one, made it to the hotel, grabbed our stuff, got the concierge to put it in storage and then rocked up here to try and recover.'

'And you think a bit of fried bread and a couple of bangers is going to help you do that? You look like extras from *Dawn of the Dead*.'

Simon chuckled. 'You can talk, fella, have you looked in the mirror lately? Bit of a late one was it?'

'You could say that,' replied Phil. 'So what's the plan? Wait out hangovers and the like here and then hop on the plane?'

'Funny you should ask,' said Simon, 'we were just talking about that when you arrived.'

'And?'

'Well, given that this is your stag weekend the conclusion we came to is that it should be up to you. Anything at all, you name it and we'll go there.'

'Anything?'

'Yeah, anything.'

'Fine,' said Phil, 'then I want to go to Vondelpark.'

'To see your dad's tree?' asked Degsy. 'I wouldn't have thought you'd be interested.'

'I'm not,' replied Phil enigmatically. 'It's just something I want to do.'

The boys responded with a variety of groans making it clear that they had in fact been hoping that Phil would be as keen to sit outside the Shamrock Inn doing as little moving as possible as they were, but when Phil said that he was happy to go on his own, they reluctantly rose as one to their feet, donned their sunglasses and followed Phil to the tram stop.

There was only one reason Phil wanted to go to Vondelpark and that was because of Sanne. She had wanted to take him there after their visit to the Van Gogh Museum and he had declined; now he wished that he could just go back in time, stop being such an idiot, and make the most of hanging out with someone like Sanne. But without a time machine to hand his only option was to take himself off to see the things she might have wanted to show him.

Vondelpark was much like any other urban green space, but just as parks in England come alive in a heat wave the same was true here. It seemed like everybody in Amsterdam from teenage boys larking about by the edge of the lake through to multi-generational families preparing barbecue lunches was out enjoying the sunshine.

The boys made a lap of the park and bought ice creams from a nearby stand and, while the majority went off with Patrick to see if they could find the very tree he claimed to have woken up in all those years ago, Phil and Simon lay down in the shade of a plane tree watching them.

Simon shook his head. 'They've got no chance have they?'

'Of finding a tree that Dad claims to have woken up in some time in the seventies?' replied Phil. 'Nah, mate. No chance.'

'And yet still they search.'

'Well, if it makes them happy.'

Simon looked up at the leaf canopy above his head. 'I've been a bit of an idiot haven't I?'

Phil joined his friend looking up at the tree. 'Yeah.'

'You were right about Caitlin, she'd never want to get back with me. It's not like she didn't make it clear enough the half a dozen times I asked her. I suppose I just didn't want to hear it.'

'So what now?'

Simon laughed. 'Now, I've screwed up my life? Not a clue.'

'Couldn't you talk to Yaz, try and maybe patch things up?'

'You think it's patchable? I screwed her over and left her and the kids to chase after Caitlin of all people! I'll be lucky if she doesn't kill me on the spot the second she hears the full story.'

'Still,' said Phil, 'what other option is there?'

'None,' replied Simon.

Phil sighed. 'Don't you sometimes wish that life was just a little less complicated?'

'Meaning yours is up the spout too?' grinned Simon. 'Last time we spoke you were minutes away from flying back to the UK, hunting down Aiden Reid and stringing him up good and proper.'

'And I nearly did,' replied Phil. 'Among the many mental things that happened to me last night I tried to get a flight back home.' Phil told Simon everything that he had learned about Aiden Reid's weekend.

Simon sat bolt upright. 'And he's there now? We should hire a plane and kill the tosser right now! What have you done about it? Have you called Helen? Tried to warn her at least?'

'And say what exactly? He's been there since Friday

night – chances are anything that he wanted to say to her has already been said. She'll already have made her decision.'

'Mate,' exclaimed Simon, 'just listen to yourself. You're giving up without a fight! Just because he's famous and loaded doesn't mean you have to roll over and admit defeat. Don't sit there feeling sorry for yourself, get up and do something!'

'Like what?'

'Like anything!'

'I've told you there's nothing I *can* do. Plus, last night it sort of got really—' Phil stopped suddenly and leapt to his feet.

Confused, Simon stood up too. 'Are you going to finish that sentence? What happened? Are you saying something happened with Sanne?'

'Forget all that for a minute!' replied Phil. 'I've got it! I've finally got it!'

'Got what?'

'One minute: nothing and then the next it was like – bam! – and it was there in my head! Helen's mobile number,' said Phil breaking into a run.

With Simon by his side Phil ran to the entrance to the park and then stopped as he remembered he and the boys had no way of contacting each other should he lose them again. He ran back to his friends, who were all standing at the base of a beech tree looking up at its branches.

'We've got to go,' panted Phil, 'I need to get something and we all have to go.'

'But we've only just found your dad's tree!' said Deano. 'It's a pretty cool one too, and look right up there in the branches: a couple of parrots! How cool is that?'

Phil shook his head in disbelief and looked. He couldn't see any parrots but this was the least of his objections. 'How can you even tell if it's the same tree? Don't you think it might have changed a little bit in the last forty-odd years?'

'It's definitely the one!' said Patrick. 'When you go to bed in a hotel and wake up in a tree my friend, believe me you remember the tree!'

'Fine! Take a snap of the tree *and* the bloody parrots if it makes you so happy and then let's go!'

Deano whipped out his digital camera and handed it to Phil while the boys and Patrick (who was beaming like he'd just won the lottery) stood with their arms around each other in front of the tree. Just as Phil pressed down on the shutter release three pale green parrots swooped down from inside the tree, rested on a branch next to his father's head as though desperate to be in the shot and then, alarmed by Patrick's yell of surprise, soared up into the safety of a nearby oak tree.

'Can we go now?'

'Go where?'

'A phone shop,' said Phil. 'I need to buy myself a phone.'

Phil ran as fast as he could back out on to the street and then stopped as he realised that he had no idea where to find a mobile phone shop.

Determined not to fall at this first hurdle Phil stopped an elderly man wearing a yellow sun hat.

'Excuse me, do you know where I can find a mobile phone shop?'

The man spoke in a flurry of dissociated consonants that Phil assumed was Dutch.

Phil explained that he didn't speak Dutch but the man just shrugged and continued on his way, so Phil ran to a group of teenage girls standing at a tram stop and asked the same question. Their immediate reaction was to giggle amongst themselves for a frustratingly long time because they were teenage girls and that's what teenage girls did whether they were from Nottingham or the Netherlands, but then one of them composed herself long enough to screech: 'There is a GSM shop, maybe three hundred metres that way!' and so Phil thanked her profusely and then ran full pelt in the direction in which she had pointed.

He almost had the shop in his sights when he came to a sudden halt. Coming down the street towards him were the guys from Essex who they'd had words with on Friday night. He counted them up; there were at least twelve to his seven if he included his dad, which he wasn't sure he should in the circumstances.

This is it, thought Phil, this is how my life is going to end: at the hands of a bunch of soft southern bricklayers.

'Look who it ain't,' called Tall Guy who had done most of the talking on the Friday night. 'It's Mr Suited and Booted and his friends. Told you we'd meet them again sooner or later.' He walked over to Phil.

'Not so hard now are you?' he spat as he pushed him in the chest.

Phil pushed him back and a scuffle of sorts ensued with both groups edging closer. Wrenching the guy's arm away from his jacket Phil managed to break free of his grip but only at the expense of his clothing. There was a loud rip as the sleeve of his jacket came loose.

'Wait!' yelled Phil as the boys rushed to his side. The last thing he needed was a fight. Phil looked at the Essex stag boys as if seeing them for the first time. Were they really all bricklayers? Were they even all from Essex? Somehow Phil doubted it. By and large they looked just like the boys, thirtysomething husbands, fathers and boyfriends all of whom no doubt had work first thing Monday morning. So okay, some of them were arseholes when they had had a skinfull, but at the end of the day these guys could easily have been people he'd call friend.

'Which one if you is getting married?' asked Phil, addressing the Essex stag boys.

'What's it to you?' barked Tall Guy.

'Listen,' said Phil, 'before this kicks off I just want to speak to him, man to man.'

'It's me,' piped up a young guy at the back of the group, 'what is it you want to say?'

Phil held up his hands in peace and walked over to the young guy, holding out his hand. 'My name's Phil. What's yours?'

'Jim,' replied the young guy, reluctantly shaking Phil's hand.

'Nice to met you, Jim. Where you from?'

'Chelmsford.'

'Cool,' said Phil. 'I hear it's nice down there, is it?'

'It's okay.'

'Well, Jim,' said Phil, 'I'm from Nottingham. I don't know if you've ever been but if you haven't you should go some time. You'll love it.'

Jim looked confused.

'Listen, Jim,' continued Phil, 'when are you getting married? Next Saturday?'

Jim nodded.

'Well that's great news,' said Phil, 'because, guess what, so am I.'

Jim said nothing.

'Now listen, Jim,' said Phil, 'I'm going to ask you a question, man to man, like, and I want you to think about it really carefully before you reply: What is your missus going to say when you come home tonight with a black eye and split lip? If she's anything like mine she is going to do her nut, isn't she? It'll be all: you've ruined what's supposed to be the best day of my life! How am I supposed to show my photos to Aunt Fanny in Australia when you look like you've just stepped out of a boxing ring! She is going to be livid isn't she?'

Jim smiled reluctantly. 'She'll blow her top, mate. My life won't be worth living.'

'Exactly,' said Phil, 'and neither will mine and given that once she gets wind of half the stuff that's happened over the weekend she'll already be borderline nuclear, winding her up any more than necessary isn't something that I'm keen to do. So why don't you tell your mate or brother or whoever it is who's got the mouth to back down and I'll back down too and we'll go our separate ways, and neither of our missuses need give us a hard time. But you if don't, I promise you as one groom to another no matter what happens to me in the process, I will make sure that come next Saturday, there won't be a single photo of your wedding day that won't remind your missus of just how much she hates you.' Phil paused. 'So what do you say? Truce?'

'Sod it,' said the young guy, holding out his hand, 'I never wanted to fight you guys in the first place.'

He called out to Tall Guy. 'Gav, yeah? Let's just leave it, okay? Straight up, the guy's cool, okay?'

Phil could barely breathe as the tall guy nodded to his friends and they left without incident. Once they were gone the boys rushed over to Phil's side.

'I thought we were goners there,' gasped Degsy. 'My whole life flashed before my eyes! What did you say to make him back down like that?'

'Nothing much,' replied Phil, 'I just appealed to his better half.' Phil fingered the gaping hole at the shoulder of his jacket, 'I'm just glad it's all over and done with because I've got a phone to buy.'

The GSM shop was pretty much like every mobile phone shop that Phil had ever been in: needlessly oversupplied with choices. A young sales assistant, with bad skin and a ridiculous haircut, sensing Phil's urgency approached him and said something in Dutch.

'Do you speak English?'

The man nodded as if Phil was an idiot. 'Yes, yes of course. My name is Mart, how can I help you today?'

'I need a phone.'

'Well that's good because we have many phones here. What sort of features were you hoping for?'

'I don't care! I really don't care. I just need a phone, any phone, that can be up and ready as soon as possible, by which I pretty much mean now.' Phil pulled out his wallet and handed the young man his credit card. 'Any pay as you go phone, I don't care which or how much as long as you can make it happen now.'

The young man walked over to his boss and began talking to him, occasionally pointing in Phil's direction. Phil worried that having quite clearly shown himself to be a nutter in a dishevelled black suit and tie on a ludicrously hot day there was every chance he might not get a phone at all but then the young man disappeared into a back office only to reappear five minutes later with a phone in his hand.

'We had this pay-as-you-go-phone up and ready in the back office with nearly ten Euros on it and can do you a deal on it if you like?'

'I'll take it,' said Phil. 'Don't bother wrapping it because I'm going to use it right now.'

Phil paid for the phone and joined the boys outside the shop. It was clear from their faces that Simon had filled in the salient information for them.

'So what are you going to say to her?' asked Deano. 'Are you going to give her what for?'

'He doesn't need to give her what for,' said Reuben. 'She hasn't done anything.'

'Yeah but, you know,' said Spencer. 'He's Aiden Reid, isn't he?'

'And Phil,' said Simon, 'is Phil Hudson, the one and only if you don't mind, and he's got something up his sleeve haven't you mate? What are you going to say to her?'

'Nothing,' said Phil. 'I'm not going to say a single word.' Phil then switched on the phone, eventually worked out how to set up text messaging, typed in Helen's number and stared at the blank screen waiting for inspiration to strike. He thought about what Simon had said earlier, he thought about the advice Sanne had given him and finally he thought about all the years he and Helen had had together. In that instant the message seemed to write itself. He pressed send and looked up at the boys with the widest of grins.

Simon spoke first.

'You done?'

Phil nodded.

'And now?'

Phil tucked the phone away in his pocket. 'Now, we go home.'

18.

The boys entered the hotel lobby for the last time. Pooling their ticket stubs together they handed them to the concierge then sat down in the reception area joking and larking about while waiting for their bags to arrive.

With all the seats taken Phil stood leaning against the wall content to watch his friends enjoying themselves. Putting the big question of everything that had happened to him personally aside for a moment, for the boys at least the past two days had been exactly what they had all needed: a break from the norm, combined with laughter on tap and plenty of opportunities to seek out trouble. It had been like the old days, back before they had wives, mortgages and kids, when every weekend had the potential to be the best weekend of their lives. And while there was no way that Phil wanted to revert to his old lifestyle, their escapades in Amsterdam had proved that the occasional relapse was no bad thing. Regardless of whether or not he would be married this time next week, he resolved that he and the boys would get another weekend together, and always take the time to remember why exactly they were all friends.

With their bags safely retrieved, there was nothing

for the boys to do but leave the hotel. Phil looked up the street in the direction of the station at various groups of young men, much like themselves, who were now making their way back home to their wives and girlfriends and to the lives they had left. For a few days the city that had briefly been their home would return to normal and its citizens would go back to work. Then come the weekend, when the first budget flights of the day hit the tarmac at Schipol Airport, the international occupation of Amsterdam would begin all over again.

The journey to the airport was uneventful. A general lack of sleep over the weekend had rendered not just the boys but pretty much the entire carriage silent, and most occupants seemed content to rest back in their seats, close their eyes and doze for the twenty-minute journey out of the city centre.

Groggy from their naps, the boys followed their fellow passengers up the escalator to the main station concourse. Reuben took charge and, once he had discovered the check-in desk, corralled the boys to the appropriate location. Much to their collective disappointment, it wasn't a case of simply handing over passports and printed e-tickets to an overly made up check-in clerk; the airline had switched to a self-service check-in area that would require the boys to use their brains.

Spencer stepped forward to the machine and began following the onscreen instructions for the inputting of his ticket number and the scanning of his passport details and while it took him two attempts to get it right, in the end he agreed it was a great deal less frustrating than he had initially thought. As a self-appointed expert he assisted each of the boys to input their details until only Phil was left.

'Right then,' said Spencer, adopting a comedy female voice straight out of Monty Python, 'would sir like to hand me his e-ticket print-out and passport?'

Amused Phil reached into his pocket and pulled out his e-ticket but his passport wasn't there.

Determined not to make a scene Phil quickly checked the pockets of his bag but when that search too proved fruitless he began to panic.

'What's up?' asked Reuben. 'You've not lost it have you?'

'Of course I haven't. It's in here somewhere I just can't lay my hands on it.'

The rest of the boys gathered around and began searching through Phil's case in a bid to help him, but it quickly became clear that the passport wasn't in the case at all.

'When did you last have it?' asked Patrick. 'Just think back to when you last saw it and work backwards from there.'

'The last time I saw it was last night wasn't it? After seeing you at the station I came here to try and get an early flight home and I definitely had it because I remember showing it to the girl on the desk.'

'So where did you go after that?'

'I took a taxi back to Amsterdam and when we reached the city centre there was some sort of traffic jam so we got out and I remember checking the back of the cab like I always do since I left my phone in a cab one time and then I'm pretty sure that I double-checked that I had the passport because I was worried about losing it and then I—' Phil stopped. He'd slept at Sanne's hadn't he? The passport could've slipped out of his jacket pocket when he'd taken it off to sleep, when he'd picked it up off the floor in the morning or even when he'd undressed to take a shower in Sanne's bathroom.

He looked at his watch. There was no way he could go all the way back to Sanne's, pick up his passport and still make the flight and he had to make the flight. He just had to. There was too much to lose if he didn't.

'I'm screwed,' said Phil. 'I'm really screwed.' Deciding that this was neither the time nor the place for a mental meltdown, Phil forced himself to consider his options and concluded that there really only was one. He pulled out his new phone hoping that he could find the piece of paper with Sanne's number, but then Simon jabbed him in the ribs. Sanne was standing straight ahead of him holding his passport in the air.

'You have no idea how glad I am to see you.'

'I think I can guess,' said Sanne and they hugged tightly. 'After I left you I cycled to Rembrandtpark to clear my head a little so by the time I got home I was so exhausted all I wanted to do was sleep the afternoon away. I was getting into bed when my foot hit something on the floor and there was your passport. I knew there was no way I'd find you unless I came to the airport.'

'I don't know what to say,' said Phil. 'I'm completely in your debt. I should give you something in return . . . I don't suppose you're in the market for some hi-fi equipment?'

Sanne laughed. 'Look, just book yourself on to your flight before they close! Once you've done that maybe I'll let you buy me a coffee.'

Phil rushed back to the check-in area, logged on to one of the terminals, booked on to the flight and, job complete, walked over to the boys.

'So?' said Deano, his voice oozing suggestively, 'the hottie from Holland had your passport? How did that happen then? Slip out somewhere did it?'

'Doesn't matter,' said Phil, 'I've got it now, that's the main thing. Listen, you guys, I need to say a proper thank you so rather than having you lot hanging around watching my every move like a bunch of overgrown school kids why don't you check in my bag for me, go through security and I'll see you on the other side.'

'If that's what you want,' said Simon, 'that's what we'll do.' He grabbed Deano by the arm. 'Come on you, show over.'

As the boys began walking away, Phil called out to his father.

'What's up?' said Patrick.

'You haven't got any more on you have you? Like I said, if they catch you again it won't just be a fine.'

Patrick sighed, pulled out a joint from his pocket and handed it to his son. 'I bought some when you disappeared earlier today to say goodbye to your friend. I had to really, fella told me it was a strain he'd come up with himself.'

Phil dropped the joint in a nearby bin and then looked over at Simon. 'Just give him the once over before you hit security will you, otherwise they really will lock him up and throw away the key.'

Once they were out of sight he walked over to Sanne. 'So how about that coffee then?'

Sanne shook her head. 'I don't think we should, do you?'

Phil grinned. 'It's just coffee.'

'No,' said Sanne, 'it's not, when it's the middle of the afternoon in a busy international airport.' They both sat down. 'Have you decided what you're going to do?'

Phil shrugged and looked over at a couple pushing a trolley piled high with suitcases. 'I know I still love her, and that's about all I know for sure. I suppose at the end of the day the rest – whether we stay together, whether we get married or not, it's up to her – I'm not the one who's changed my mind. I'm still the guy who wants to spend the rest of my life with her.'

'That's good, that's exactly the kind of thing she'll need to hear.'

'If it's so good then why do I feel so bad? I know something happened between them. I can feel it right at the centre of my gut. And part of me wants to punish her and part of me wants to beg her to stay and I just don't get what the right thing is to do here.' He stopped and looked directly at Sanne. 'I mean last night . . . I could have ruined everything.'

'But you didn't and that's the important thing, if I'd thought, even for a moment that you didn't really love her . . .'

Phil grinned. 'You mean I could have been in with a shot with Sanne from Misty Mondays? How cool would that have been?'

Sanne threw her arms around him for what he was sure would be their final embrace. 'I don't get it,' said Phil. 'I'm not a singer, or a DJ or even an actor, I'm just an ordinary bloke from Nottingham who runs a hi-fi shop and you're . . . well you're you. How could I have ever stood a chance with you?'

'What can I say?' replied Sanne, with a grin, 'I'm just a sucker for a man in a suit.'

Phil looked into her eyes. In a few moments he would never see her again and Sanne must have had the same thought because she tilted her head up and placed her lips firmly against Phil's. It was all over in a matter of seconds, and although the line that Phil had fought so hard not to cross had been transgressed, this time he felt no guilt at all.

Sanne tapped Phil lightly on the chest with the palm of her hands. 'You should go,' she said quietly, 'or you'll miss the plane.'

He didn't move.